The BASILISK Queen

the lasina chronicles   book two

By Rozie Marshall

Enchanted Embers Press
PO BOX 585
Castle Rock, Colorado 80104

ISBN: 979-8-9857077-4-8 (Paperback)
ISBN: 979-8-9857077-3-1 (Hardcover)
ISBN: 979-8-9857077-5-5 (eBook)

Library of Congress Control Number: 2022904994

Any references to historical events, real people, or real places are used fictitiously. Names, characters, and places are products of the author's imagination.

Front cover image by Pixie Covers
Book design by Enchanted Embers Press
Printed by IngramSpark, in the United States of America.
Edited by Max Williams with BBB Publishing

First Enchanted Embers Press printing edition 2022.
www.roziemarshall.com

Contents

IV

VI

Dedication

To all the women who love sex, sin, and just a touch of scales.

Mindy G and Krystal; I hope all your fantasies come true with this series. Please stop sending me pictures of your snakes, they scare the shit out of me.

To my husband; Thanks for indulging my curiosity on reptile mating habits and maybe twisting them for the purposes of this series.

To Everly Taylor, thank you for all the invaluable information on reptiles.

Thank you to all my readers for the love and support you give me; without you this wouldn't be possible.

Thank you brain for the Ophidiophobia and the very realistic nightmares I could

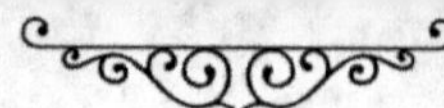

VIII

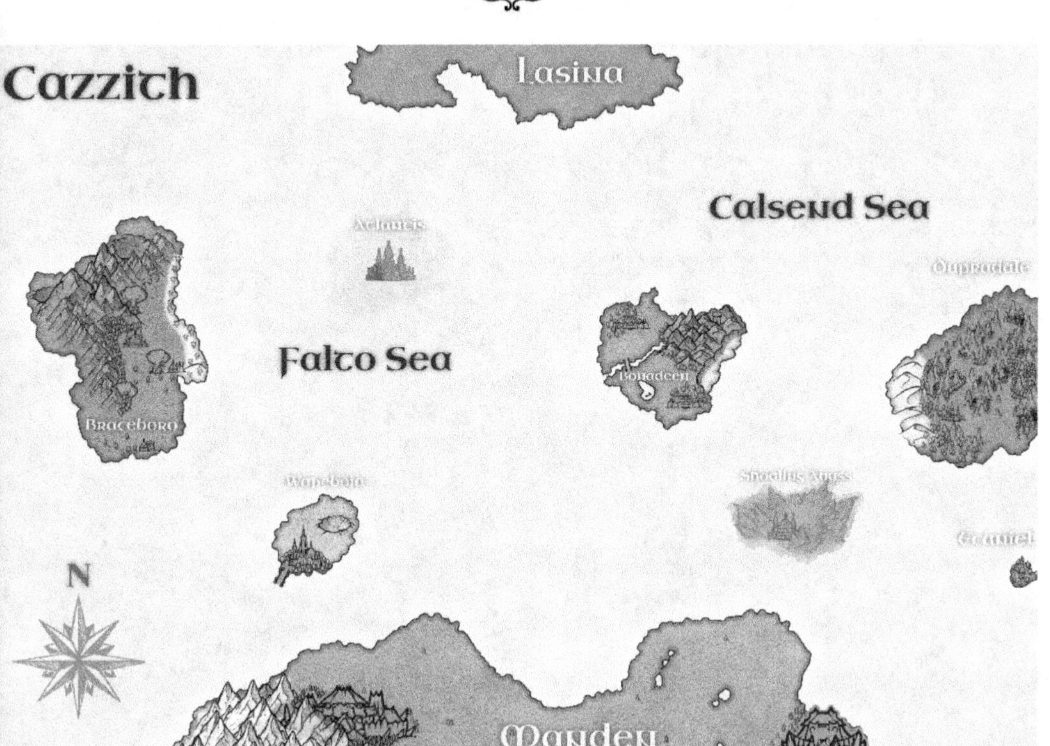

Cazzich
Lasina
Calsend Sea
Falco Sea
Braceboro
Bonadeen
N
Manden
IX

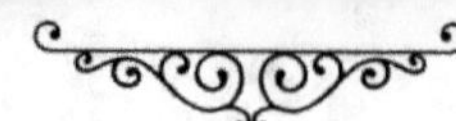

X

Lasina
Northern Kingdom
Eastern Kingdom
Western Kingdom
Southern Kingdom
Cave
Merfolk
Nymph Lake
Vago's Carriage
Gryphon Grove
Sprites
Mimic Grove
N

XII

Sierin

"WHAT DO YOU MEAN SHE'S GONE?" I yelled at the head guard on this trip. "HOW IN THE FUCK DID YOU LOSE HER?"

"Ajih, was with her in the market and a boy bumped into Her Majesty. Ajih ran after the boy and Her Majesty disappeared," The guard spoke, defending himself as we stood in the inn. "I have sent the others out to find her, Your Highness. Ajih is here and knows she must be punished for her miscalculation."

"Miscalculation... MISCALCULATION!" Kai roared, and the guard trembled slightly in the face of his wrath. "GET OUT, FIND HER." The guard rushed out the door to hopefully join the hunt for Maisie.

"Kai, get the unicorns saddled up, Emot fly back and get the Eastern Kingdom guards, and have them fan out to find her." Emot and Kai raced from the room, Emot shifting as soon as the door was open. "Zugo, since you are still weak you should stay here, Cobra can stay and help you get better. Viper, will you help us find her?"

"I don't need to help you find her, she is with her father, heading North through the Carlenan Woods. His carriage is swift,

but not fast enough to outrun a unicorn at full speed. Take the Dawnroad Trail, you can cut them off." I watched in awe as her eyes faded back to their original grey-blue color. "Don't ask."

I nodded once and raced down the stairs to join Kai, he was already mounted up. Tossing the reins of the second unicorn next to me, I wheeled around and raced towards the Dawnroad Trail, Kai right beside me. Once away from the village, I let my unicorn have its free reins and we flew along the open road. I began to hear the sound of rushing wind as we raced along.

Kai kept pace the entire way, watching the skies for the winged guard. I heard him point and yell as we neared the far side of the wood, while Emot swooped down to fly beside me. "I sssaw a carriage racing through the woodsss towardsss the Rugnora Passss, the guardsss won't make it in time we need to hurry." He flew ahead and I let my mount go even faster. We needed to get to the pass before they did, or she would be lost to us forever.

The trees raced by as we sped along, the colors blurring together, then the pass was in sight. Emot was perched on a high rock watching the road from the west, as a carriage raced towards us. I could hear the sound of a whip cracking as they raced along the road, dirt dusting the air. I veered off, heading directly towards them, jumping from my unicorn's back when I was close enough to hit the driver head on.

I shifted in midair and snapped my jaws around his throat before he could think about shifting. After snuffing the life out of the driver, I broke the rail and leather that held the unicorns locked to the carriage, and they continued to race ahead, no longer burdened by the load. Kai and Emot took out the guards around us, but then I heard the sound of wood breaking.

A massive green basilisk broke through the carriage walls, Maisie dangling from his tail. He didn't bother attacking us just

rushed towards the pass. I went to follow when something hit me in the back of the head forcing me to shift back into human form. I looked around but didn't see anything. Emot and Kai raced after, but as I watched them, two more bottles of glowing black liquid hit them forcing their shifts as well. Just as we began to run, while trying desperately to shift, Maisie screamed out for help.

Maisie

    I screamed as the green basilisk tightened around me, my bag digging into my stomach. Wriggling my arms free, I pounded on his scales, and my father just laughed maniacally, as he kept going. Behind me, I heard the sounds of yelling and looked around. Emot and Kai were running behind me, yelling. Racking my brain, I tried to find a way out of Vago's grip.

    A whisper on the wind reached my ears, "*The knife I gave you silly girl.*" Viper's voice sounded in my head and I pulled my bag out of Vago's coil. Ripping it open as fast as I could, the camera flew out and shattered on the ground, as Vago continued into a large cliff canyon. I rummaged my hand around and felt the dagger slice the side of my hand, grabbing it I pulled it free. Tossing my bag to the ground behind us, I gripped the dagger's handle with both hands and plunged it into Vago's scales.

    The speed at which he released me was blinding, and I hit the ground hard. I got up and ran away as fast as my legs could carry me. Without warning, I found myself scooped up from above, and was flying over the open ground. As we flew, I saw Emot and Kai on the ground still running, The basilisk that had me swooped landing low just before them, and then let me go.

    Several more guards dropped in, surrounding us. Emot pulled me to his chest and hugged me tight. "Why did you leave?"

He asked, as Kai pulled me from his arms to wrap me in a hug of his own.

Sic ran up and pulled me from Kai's grip. "We need to go now, back to Mistshore." We turned to the guards and they began to pick us up one by one, then we were flying South. I looked back towards the large canyon behind us and saw a lone man gazing after us as we flew off. While I watched, a woman slipped out of the rock wall and joined him, standing close by his side.

We landed back in Mistshore on the docks near the inn, only to have Viper walk out of the main door. "Seriously, girl." She pulled me by the arm into the building and up the stairs. Throwing the door open against the far wall, she pushed me through before slamming it shut again. "You almost got them killed. If Cobra hadn't forced them to shift back, they would have been dead right now," She hissed at me. Cobra slithered into the room from the window and shifted.

Zugo was asleep on the bed by the wall and Cobra ignored me to check his eyes. "You have five minutes before he comes too, I can't make the others forget you ran, Viper might." She said as she looked at her sister. "Zugo, at least won't know that you left at all, and that is a good thing." Cobra put her hand out and snapped her fingers. "Your hand." I placed mine in hers and watched as she healed my cut as if it never happened. "Tell anyone I did that, and I'll kill you myself."

The others entered the room and froze, as Viper turned towards them. "Too many guards saw, hiding sex is one thing, but I can't shield you from this. The only thing I can do is make sure Zugo doesn't find out." She released whatever hold on them she had and spoke to them directly, "Zugo won't remember that she

left, try to keep it that way. There is another room that you can use to yell at her."

The fury on Sic's face scared me as Emot pulled me back out of the room, and down the hallway. They entered a different room, Sic barely waiting for the door to close before he started yelling, "How could you run off like that? Don't you know he would have killed you without a care? The guards found Sam's body, along with this," He held up a necklace, the one I had gotten in the market. He shoved it into his pocket, angrily running a hand through his hair.

Turning away. Sic began to pace. I looked at Kai, who had an equally pissed look on his face, as he shook his head. Emot, on the other hand, look hurt, betrayed, as if I had crushed his heart and it would never recover. "I just wanted to go home," I whispered into the silence, feeling like a recalcitrant child in the face of their anger.

"Don't you get it yet? This is your home now," Sic said, while rubbing the bridge of his nose in frustration. "I don't mean to sound like an ass about it, but the likelihood that your mother survived is slim, and if she did, she would come back here for you." Sic's words sliced through my chest and I couldn't breathe. The only thing that had been holding me together was getting home.

"We need to go. The guards can fly us back to the castle. She isn't safe here, and if he knows we came back here then he might attack," Kai's words were directed at Sic. All I could do was sit on the chair in the corner, thinking about how Sic was probably right.

I felt the first tear roll down my face and tried to stop the others, but they kept coming. Looking out the window to hide it from them, I noticed Emot's reflection in the glass. He looked

miserable, and I realized, my leaving had hurt him. My selfish actions had caused so much trouble, and now I had to face the music.

A knock on the door stopped Sic's pacing. He swung it wide as a guard bowed low. "Everyone is ready to leave, Your Highness." Sic nodded, and they waited for me to stand. I didn't bother looking at anything but the floor as I marched outside, once more. Zugo, Viper, and Cobra, all sat waiting on the backs of guards, while others waited for us to join them. Kai picked me up and placed me on the back of one. there were straps to hold on to that he handed me, then I was soaring through the air.

The others caught up quickly, and we made it back to the castle in half the time it had taken us to get there. Once back at the castle, the guards landed in the main courtyard letting us off. I didn't bother waiting for anyone, I just walked in through the main castle doors and up the stairs. More guards opened doors for me as I entered my room, heading straight for my bathroom. Turning the lock on the bathroom door, I slid down the wood panel and began sobbing.

What had I done? My mother was probably dead, now Sam was, too. Despite the fact that he had hurt me so badly, several times, I hadn't wanted him dead. I had broken Emot's heart when I had run off, and Zugo didn't even know I had been gone, so I had to lie to him. The tears just kept coming, not in self-pity, but self-hatred, I couldn't even stand myself at the moment. My basilisk tried to comfort me some, but she was feeling just as guilty about my actions as I was.

I heard the guys on the other side of the door, but didn't bother opening it. How could I expect them to ever forgive me, knowing how much I had hurt them? I laid on the floor as the sunset outside, the room growing dark around me. My tears

eventually stopped, the sounds of life eventually quieted, and I fell asleep on the cold tile floor.

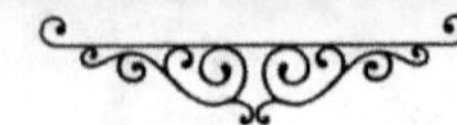

2

Maisie

When I woke, a few hours later, the bathroom was still pitch black. I rose and found the light switch, flipping the light on. I was still in awe that some things were just like home, and yet, others were totally different. The bright light hurt my eyes as it illuminated the room, and I made my way over to the sink. Splashing cool water over my face to hopefully get rid of any puffiness, I gazed at the mirror.

"You're a stupid, stupid girl," I told my reflection. "You need to put your big girl panties on and do what's right. That means marriage, mating, and whatever else they tell you. Forget about Earth, Mom is dead so there is nothing to go back to now, anyway." Drying my face on a towel, I unlocked the door and stepped out into the room. I noticed Sic's door was fully repaired, as I walked towards the sitting area through the big double door.

The sitting area was just as quiet, and the fire in the grate burned low. I walked out of the room and down towards the stairs, the night guards bowing as I passed. My stomach rumbled as I reached the main floor and decided to go to the kitchens. The spiral stairs were softly lit with the wall sconces as I made my way down into the kitchen. Once I hit the bottom step, I noticed a low light coming from the fridge.

Slowly entering the room, I watched Emot close the fridge. He turned and placed several things on the counter before noticing me standing there. "Do you want sssomething?" His words were cold and emotionless, making me realize how much I had hurt him.

"I just came to grab a snack, but I'll leave you alone." I turned to leave, not wanting to hurt him more.

"You don't have to go. Thisss issss your home, you're allowed to go wherever you want," He spoke softly, and I paused in the entryway.

"I don't want to bother you. I'll just grab something and go back to the room." I turned back and walked to the fridge, swiftly opening the door to see what I could grab quickly, then I would leave. I could feel Emot's eyes on my back as I looked. Reaching for a yogurt, I felt his hand on my side and froze.

His warmth wrapped around me as he stepped closer and pulled the door from my light grip. Closing it, his other hand wrapped around my waist and he pulled me back fully against his chest. My breathing hitched as tears welled in my eyes, the comfort he gave me, unwillingly breaking my resolve to stay away from him.

"Why did you run? And why with him?" His whisper was soft, and I could hear the pain in his voice. A tear rolled down my cheek and I harshly wiped it away, refusing to cry more.

"I just wanted to go home, and he said he had a way to get back to Earth. I knew he was lying about wanting us to get back together, but I didn't care what excuse he gave me, if it got me back to my mom." I paused for a moment taking a deep breath before I said the next part, "Sic is right, though, and my mom is probably dead."

He pulled my hair off my shoulder and I sighed. "It was never about getting back with him?" His question caressed my skin as his breath touched my shoulder.

I shook my head 'no' and spoke softly, "He cheated on me. I do have some dignity." His lips pressed to my shoulder and I felt a tear leak out of the corner of my eye.

"Then why did the guardsss find a necklace near hisss body? Did he give it to you?" My head dropped to the side a his mouth worked its way up to my ear.

"A vendor in the market gave it to me, as a gift." I moaned softly as his teeth scraped my earlobe. "She said it was for protection, from what, she didn't say. I can't even remember what she called it. Acid-something," He sucked hard as I explained, before stepping back, turning me in the process.

"Assssitrine?" He asked as he picked me up, spun around, and placed me on the counter.

"Yes, that's it. What is it anyway?" I asked, as he spread my legs and stepped between them.

"Do you really want me to talk about gemsss?" He asked, as he pulled me against his body before dropping a kiss to my lips. "Or, would you rather I do thisss?" He ground his hips into my core, causing my head to drop back.

"Emot, we shouldn't." He paused at my words, and I felt his hand slide up my back cradling my head.

"Why not? You are my wife, ssso why can't I feassst on you?" The possessive way he said wife had me aching to let him touch me, but I knew he would regret it. I had hurt him and that wasn't something he would get over quickly.

13

His other hand slid down the front of my clothes and up under my shirt cupping the underside of my breast. It was hard to focus on what the right thing to do was when he was tantalizingly close and touching my skin. "Because I hurt you, and it wouldn't be right."

"I'm not sssome naive kid Maissie. I'm well aware of what I'm doing and why I'm doing it. Yesss, you hurt me, but only becaussse I thought you wanted to leave with him. If you had asked, Sssic would have made a portal for you to go sssee your mother, or at least check to sssee if ssshe was alive or not." He pulled my shirt up and off gazing into my eyes. "I wasssn't hurt becaussse you wanted to go home, it isss natural to missss home. I was hurt becaussse you're mine, oursss, not hissss. Call me a posssesssive asssshole but we've loved you for longer, and while you were unaware, it ssstill hurt to have to lisssten to the two of you. And now that I've had you, I won't let you go."

He pulled his own shirt off and tossed it to the floor. His scales began to cover his chest and his eyes changed shape, the pupils elongating like those of a snake. "Even my basssilisssk knowsss you're oursss," His hiss becoming even more apparent as his tongue forked. He leaned me back onto the counter, knocking the food to the floor in the process. His tongue flicked out and teased my nipple to an aching peak. He didn't pull my pants off as I expected, and didn't remove his either.

"Emot, please," I whispered, and he lifted his head to look at me.

"I can't, not right now, not if you want fully human, I'm not in control enough." My basilisk hissed at me as she pushed outwards, scales rising across my breasts. My vision changed and I could taste his scent, and his hand caressed my body. I said fuck it and let her take over, what happened, happened. Emot hissed as I reached down to unbutton his pants. "Maisssssie, sssstop, I'm not

in control." He grabbed my hand to stop me, but I didn't stop. With my other hand, I pulled him in for a hard kiss.

I pushed his pants off his hips and wrapped my hand around first, one cock, then the other. He broke our kiss swiftly, "Fuck." I couldn't agree more, as I stroked him again. His hands went to my own pants and he had them ripped off within seconds, pulling my hands out of the way in the process. His body was covered in scales just like mine was, and I marveled at how beautiful they were. The dark grey was the perfect backdrop for the gold and orange highlights.

He pulled me to the edge of the counter and slid his massive cock in. Pleasure shot straight through me and I cried out, as he leaned over me to recapture my nipple once again. His thrusts were hard and fast, and all I could do was hold on with my legs. I felt him bite me before kissing the sting away, and I arched off the counter. He reached above me and grabbed the end of the counter pulling himself up over me, while sliding me back more. We used his grip to polish the marble with my body and I shattered around him. Without warning, I felt my shift rip through me forcing Emot's as well. "Fuck." His tail wrapped tight to mine as we rolled onto the floor.

I could feel the soft barbs on his hemipenes, and felt my body clamp down around him. His body was wrapped around mine holding me in place while he undulated. "Emot!" My cry was a plea, and question all in one.

"Ssshift back, I can't sssshift until you do." My basilisk wouldn't release her hold as he kept moving, my body accepting his every barb and loving it. I focused on shifting and began to feel my upper half return to normal. His arms wrapped around me tightly, holding me, as his tail continued to roll. "That'ssss it."

He rolled over me and I grabbed his biceps hard. "I told you I wasn't in control," His whisper brushed my forehead as his lower half flexed harder. My body exploded in pleasure and I saw his fangs descend as he swelled inside me. The barbs holding him tight in my body felt beyond amazing, and the pulsing kept my own pleasure going. I felt his tail pull mine tighter against him as Emot pressed a kiss to my lips, then I felt my legs shift back along with his, his cocks still buried in my pussy.

I almost cried when he pulled out and rolled onto his back next to me, panting to catch his breath. "I'm sssorry." He turned to look at me and I could see the sincerity in his eyes.

"I'm not," I said, as I gazed back at him. The feel of something cold on my back had me sitting up slightly. I tried to reach the offending item, but failed. Sitting up further, I heard Emot bust out laughing, and turned to glare at him. "What?"

"You have a piece of cheessse ssstuck to your back." His laughter intensified and I couldn't help but join in. He peeled it off and tossed it towards the trash can in the corner, but missed, hitting the wall where it stuck. "Do you ssstill want sssomething to eat?" He asked as he sat up and wrapped his arms around me, pressing a kiss to my shoulder.

My stomach rumbled at his mention of food, and he smiled against my skin. Rising from the floor he began to salvage what had been knocked off in our counter encounter. Once he picked up what could still be used, he held out a hand to me, helping me stand. He pulled me to his chest and kissed me, his fangs had receded, and both of our skin had returned to normal.

"What would you like to eat?" His question was punctuated with kisses, and I giggled as I felt his cocks begin to rise again.

"You are incorrigible. How about you make us a sandwich, and I will start on an appetizer," I slowly lowered to my knees while I spoke, and grabbed his hips pulling him forward. Leaning my back on the lower cabinets, I stroked him, looking up his body. "One might be easier." He smiled and shifted them to one. "If you stop making the sandwich, I stop, too." I licked the tip and he shuttered.

"Deal," He said as he slowly began to pull out bread to slice. I listened to him slowly make us a sandwich, while I sucked him as far as I could into my throat. His groan made me repeat the action several times. At one point, I felt his hand tangle in my hair but still heard him making food, so I didn't stop. I marveled that he could make a sandwich one-handed.

"Gods damned, Emot, it smells like sex in here, were you and Sic..." Without warning the overhead light flipped on, and I heard Kai's voice trail off as he noticed Emot's hand and the look on his face. "Are you really jerking off in the kitchen while making a sandwich?" Kai laughed, and I rose so I could just see over the counter.

Kai's eyes instantly went to mine and he laughed, "Well, well, well, what do we have here?"

Emot groaned as I stroked him one last time and slowly stood trying to find my shirt. I saw it on the far side of the island and swore internally, caught naked, my pants ripped to shreds, and my shirt across the room. Kai walked forward and picked up my shirt. "Looking for this?" He teased, as he held it just out of reach. "It's gonna cost you..." he tapped his chin as he thought, "One kiss," he smiled, and then I heard his mumbled, "on my dick."

A kiss I would give, but he wasn't getting it where he wanted it most, so I stood tall. Emot cut the sandwich and handed

me a half on a plate, before putting everything away. I carried my plate around the island and stopped in front of Kai, a smug smile hung on his lips as he held my shirt out of reach. Pulling his head down I kissed him sweetly, and then whispered, "You can keep the shirt." I walked around him and up the stairs, hearing Emot's laughter as I went.

3

Maisie

I could hear Emot and Kai arguing good naturedly, as they followed me up the stairs. While it had been awkward to walk around the castle guards naked, they had all averted their eyes towards the ceiling, while still opening doors. it had been kind of funny. Sic was standing by the fire in the sitting room when I walked in with a huge smile across my face. He looked up at me and my smile dimmed as the look on his face drained some of my joy.

Kai and Emot stopped just behind me as I stood frozen in the doorway. Kai took the plate from my hand and handed me my shirt, so I could cover up. That's when I noticed Zugo sitting on the window seat. I pulled my shirt on swiftly, as Kai set my plate on the table and walked into the bedroom. He returned with a robe for me and Emot, then went to sit on the couch.

After wrapping the robe around myself, I tied it off and went to sit down. My appetite diminished somewhat as they all stood around, waiting for what, I didn't know. "You can eat, Maisie," Sic said, as he turned back to the fire. I noticed a necklace hanging from his hand as he stood there.

Emot sat down next to me and handed me his plate, while reaching for the other one on the table. "Eat, you need food." I

about rolled my eyes at him, but my stomach growled at the sight of food.

"We agreed that Zugo has a right to know what happened, so I filled him in while you two were downstairs," Sic's words were soft, and I looked over at Zugo who just shrugged. "I want you to understand the ramifications of your actions. Twelve guards are currently being punished for your actions in running away. Two were injured while attempting to help rescue you, and people died. Not good people, but people, nonetheless." He placed the necklace on the mantel rubbing his eyes and the bridge of his nose. "We are trying to create peace in this country, Maisie, not incite a war."

"Sssic take it easssy on her will you, ssshe didn't intend to get captured," Emot spoke up, and Sic glared at him.

"No, just to fucking run off with that sleaze," His voice rose slightly, and he tossed the necklace at Emot hitting him in the chest.

Emot picked up the necklace and handed it to me. "I got it from a vendor in the market. She gave it to me, ask the guard that was with me if you don't believe me." Sic, apparently, didn't believe me and walked to the door. I couldn't hear his whispers to the guards, but one scurried off.

He returned to the fire as Emot ate his sandwich, and Kai tried to get me to eat mine. I took a small bite before he took a massive one of his own. While we waited, Kai shared a bite of my sandwich, eating most of it. We waited about ten minutes before a knock sounded on the door and Sic yelled, "Enter."

Two guards entered with Ajih cuffed between them, and then stopped just inside the doorway. "Your Majesty, Your

Majesty, Your Highness, Your Highness, Your Grace." They all bowed each of us individually as Sic walked towards them.

Sic held up the necklace and asked Ajih where I had received it. "A vendor in the Mistshore Market gave it to her, Your Highness. She said it was a gift, for protection. this was before the young boy bumped into Her Majesty," Ajih spoke softly, but the room was so quiet we could all hear her words.

"Thank you, take her back." He watched them go before turning back to the rest of us. I couldn't help the smug smile that crossed my face, as he walked back and placed the necklace on the table. "I'm sorry."

"Well, now that's settled, I think we should go back to bed." Kai placed the plate on the table and bent to pick me up. Tossing me over his shoulder, he yelled back, "I call the big bed," He yelled back as he walked into the bedroom and tossed me onto the bed.

"Kai, piss off," Emot said, as he tossed his robe in Kai's face and slid in the bed next to me.

"How about you both go back to your rooms and I sleep in my bed alone," I said, as Kai untangled himself from the robe. Once free, he pouted and gave me big sad puppy dog eyes. "No, I mean it, both of you go."

Emot crawled out of the bed and pulled Kai with him. Pushing Kai into his room he closed the door on Kai. "You sssure you don't want me to ssstay?" He asked, as Zugo and Sic walked towards their own rooms.

"You heard the lady, your own bed, Emot," Sic called, as he opened his own door. Zugo laughed at Emot's expense before closing his own door. Emot walked to his room, blowing me a kiss

before very slowly inching the wood that would separate us closed. "Good night Maisie, I really am sorry," Sic spoke softly, as he turned into his own room. Once they were all shut, I flopped back onto the bed and pulled the covers over me, hoping to get some sleep.

The viper's fangs pierced my hand, injecting venom into my system as I tried to shake it free. Sic watched on as the venom slowly began to poison my body, not bothering to help. I shook my hand furiously, trying to dislodge the snake, but it wouldn't release its grip. Picking up a rock, I smashed it on the head, and it let go, only to transform into thousands of tiny snakes. They began crawling up the walls of the room and I screamed out. Emot yelling for me to follow him as he ran from the room.

I climbed onto a chair as the room slowly began filling with more and more snakes. Kai jumped back from the doorway as they began to spill into the next room. They began crawling over my feet as kicked and screamed, some wrapping themselves around me. The chair began to shake as the weight of the snakes overwhelmed the frame and then cracked. Dropping me into the mass of snakes below.

"Maisie, Maisie. Shit, she's burning up. Go get my mother," I vaguely heard Sic's voice, as I fought the snakes crawling on my skin. Hands tried to pin me down as I thrashed, the sheets sticking to my skin.

"Viper," I called out hoarsely, trying to pry my dry lips open.

"Don't get Salima, get Cobra and Viper," Emot spoke up. "What? She wants Viper, and Cobra did help Zugo."

I heard footsteps running around and then I heard Cobra's soft voice, "Everything is going to be fine, Maisie, we're here. Help sit her up." I couldn't open my eyes to see who helped me, but the sensation of snakes crawling on my skin wouldn't disappear. "Maisie, you need to drink this," Emot's voice was in my ear, as a cup was held up to my lips.

The smell of orange and ginger hit my nose and I sipped a tiny bit, the bitter taste made me gag slightly. Emot and Cobra made me drink more until I got all of the nasty liquid down. My whole body ached, and I began to feel an odd oozing feeling between my legs. "Eww, what is that?" No one moved the sheet to find out and thank the gods my eyes were still hard to open, because I didn't want to see what happened.

"When a female basilisk gets sick, her body will expel all um... semen to prevent any contamination," Emot whispered into my ear and I cringed, it was so much worse than just standing up and having it run down your leg. "Sic, Kai, and Zugo aren't here, just me, Cobra, and Viper." I felt a cool rag brush my forehead as he spoke a bit louder, relieved that I wouldn't have to deal with all of them.

"We kinda expected it, so I sent them out," Cobra's voice was no-nonsense, and I was happy to have her here. "Why didn't you want Salima here, if I might ask?"

"I don't know, she just... I don't feel comfortable with her around," I tried to explain my feelings, but the words just wouldn't come out right.

"It's fine love, we are here, and we will take care of you. Can you open your eyes yet?" Emot held me upright, so I was reclining on his chest. I tried to pry my eyes open, but they wouldn't respond. The only blessing in this situation was that it didn't feel like snakes were crawling all over me anymore.

"No, but the snakes crawling on my skin are gone." Cobra pulled the sheet back and sighed.

"She has Serpent Blight. The feeling goes away once the rash stops moving. We need to check your eyes, but I think they swelled shut, meaning you had an allergic reaction to the rash. The turmeric tea should help the inflammation but you're going to have to drink another cup." Cobra wiped the warm cloth off my head before replacing it with another cooler cloth. Emot wrapped his arms around me and rocked softly as they worked. Another cup touched my lips and the smell alone made me gag.

"Please no, it's so gross," I pleaded, and Emot stopped rocking.

"You need to drink it love or it will take days to get the swelling to go down. Just think about something else, something salty perhaps." Viper snorted in the background as Cobra tipped the cup and I tried to just let it go down.

Once I drained the cup, I tried to elbow Emot but didn't have the strength, so I just grunted, "Not funny." I heard Cobra and Viper snort softly in tandem, and then giggled. "Okay, it was kinda funny."

Emot resumed his soft rocking as Cobra placed a cool cloth across my chest and neck. Then I felt her check my eye gingerly with her fingertips. "Try to open them now." I did as she asked and cracked my eyes open. The world was blurry and bright, but I could get them open a touch. "We may have to do more if that's the furthest you can open them."

"No, please, no more of that nasty stuff," I begged, and she sighed.

"Fine, we will give it a few more minutes to work but if you can't open them fully in ten, you're drinking more." I shuddered at her words and prayed that they would open fully by then. Closing them again I felt the cool cloth placed on my forehead and eyes, and we waited.

Ten minutes passed swiftly, and the rag was removed. "Well, the swelling seems better, let's see those green eyes," Cobra cooed, and once again I tried to open them, praying they would open all the way. The room was still blurry, but I could make out where Viper was handing Cobra things on the side of the bed. "You got lucky. Can you see me?"

"Yes, but you're blurry as fuck." I waved my hand around until I touched her, and she laughed.

"The blurry vision will go away soon. Let's get you cleaned up and the sheets changed. Emot, can you have a maid change the sheets while we get her bathed?" Viper asked, as Emot worked his way out from behind me. He scooped me up and carried me into the bathroom before setting me down on the edge of the bath.

"I'll get someone to clean up the bed once you're in the tub. Cobra and Viper can help you bathe." He kissed my forehead as the bath water started and then helped me strip. Once the tub was full, he helped me sit in the water and then left, closing the door softly behind him.

Kai

Emot walked out of the room and headed straight for the outer doors, his shirt was stuck to his skin. He opened the door and asked the guards to send a maid up and then closed it again. Sic was pacing by the fire, while Zugo sat on the couch. I was in the window seat, impatiently waiting for the news on how Maisie was doing. "So, how is she?" Sic asked, as Emot flopped onto the couch next to Zugo.

"Ssshe hasss Ssserpent Blight. The ssswelling in her eyesss hasss gone down, and the rasssh looksss bad, but it hasss sssstopped moving. Ssshe ssshould be good in a day or two," Emot said, as he scrubbed a hand over his head.

"Why did you send us out?" I asked, hurt that we couldn't be helping as well.

Sic rolled his eyes and looked at me. "Really?"

"What happensss when a female basssilisssk getssss sssick?" Emot asked, and I had to think back to school when we were learning reproduction.

"Oh... OHHHH. Yep, good call, man. Good call." I felt like an idiot for about half a second until Zugo spoke up.

"What happens when a female basilisk gets sick?" He looked at me and then the other two.

I didn't care if it was childish, but I stuck two fingers in my ears and said as loud as I could. "La, la, la, not listening."

Emot looked at me. "Ssshe isss technically your wife, and I doubt ssshe isss going to be healthy all the time." I pulled my fingers out of my ears and shuddered as Sic began to speak.

"When a female basilisk gets sick, their bodies expel all of the male fluids they have stored for reproduction." Well, at least he put it scientifically, I would've just said all the jizz comes out.

"Huh, females store what?" Zugo's confusion was almost funny if it had been real. We tended to forget that he had been locked up at a young age and was barely older than Maisie.

"What do you know about reproduction?" Sic asked, and I put my head in my hands.

I was about to leave when a maid entered carrying fresh sheets. "Saved by the maid," Sic glared at my words, as she hurried through and closed the doors.

"You should be more understanding. He was in a prison. The least you can do is have the decency to help if he has questions," Sic spoke to me, before turning back to Zugo.

"I know the basics of what goes where, thanks to my uncle and the whores he kept," Zugo said in response to Sic's earlier question.

"Females store sperm for reproductive purposes, and it can remain alive for up to five years. When a female gets sick or when she is about to clutch, lay eggs, her body expels any unused male

fluids. During laying, this is when the egg gets fertilized, as it slides through the semen a sperm will enter the egg, then the egg is laid. In about sixty days babies hatch. In the case of illness, it is to prevent contamination of unfertilized eggs that are about to be laid. Although Maisie better not have any of those." He paused to glare at Emot. "It is a normal function. During egg laying it also helps lubricate the eggs, so the female doesn't get egg bound."

Zugo looked even more confused than before and I sighed. "The jizz comes out to lube things up for eggs while the litter swimmers fight to get in," I said, and his face cleared.

"Why didn't you just say that?" Zugo looked at me and smiled.

Sic pinched the bridge of his nose with his fingers as Viper came out of the room. "The bedding has been changed, and she's all cleaned up. Emot, we can get her settled back in bed, and then you can all come in."

Emot rose and followed Viper into the other room as the maid slipped out, taking the old sheets with her. Once she left, I couldn't help but laugh, "Talk about a wet spot."

"Gods, give me patience, Kai if you say one more asinine thing, I'm throwing you out for the night," Sic gritted his teeth as he spoke, and I couldn't help myself.

"Oh, *cum* now Sic, you love cream pies," I emphasized the word cum, so he grasped my meaning. "*Cum* for fun, stay for pie."

Zugo joined in as Sic marched towards me. "I didn't see that *cumming*."

I stood up and walked around the couch, putting some space in between Sic and me. "I think the time has *cum* for me to leave."

Zugo snorted as Sic began to chase me around the room. "*Cum* on man, *sperm* jokes are *nut* funny."

Sic growled at me and I ran faster. "But they just *cum* naturally to me."

Viper opened the door to see Sic chasing me around the room and gaped. "What is going on in here?"

"Ahh, the time has *cum*," I said, ducking as Sic threw a book from the table at me.

"Is she *cumming* around?" Zugo asked, and Sic stopped in front of Viper.

"These two are not allowed in the room. I'm gonna kill them." She hid her smile but nodded.

"I'm so glad I learned to masturbate... it's really going to *cum* in *handy*," I shot at his back, and he threw his hands up in the air, as Viper busted out laughing. She jerked her head towards the room, and we walked towards the door.

"Try to not be childish in there," She said, as I walked by.

"*Cum* on, you thought it was funny." I earned a slap upside the head while Zugo laughed.

5

Maisie

I watched Viper slap Kai upside the head, and I arched a brow at them as they walked closer. Sic looked annoyed and Emot sat on the side of the bed and whispered to me, "If I know Kai, he was deliberately annoying Sic, just because." He slid closer to me and plumped my pillows. My vision was still slightly blurry, but I could at least tell who was who.

Sic sat next to Emot, while Zugo and Kai took the other side of the bed. "How are you feeling, sugar?" Kai asked, as he leaned against my pillows. His head was next to me as he smiled innocently up at me.

"Why do I suspect that innocent smile is totally false, and I'm fine now, or will be." I looked at Kai and fluffed his hair a bit.

"I'm so sorry, Maisie, I didn't mean to get you sick." Zugo twisted his hands together in the comforter, looking younger than he had on the ship.

"I'm okay, really, and Viper said it's better to get it now than later." I didn't mention that she said it was better now than when my own kids caught it. That was still a bit away, in the future. I was just starting to get used to them, and kids were a huge step in my mind.

Cobra seemed to sense when my mood changed and became a mother hen once more. "Ok, Maisie needs sleep, and Zugo, so do you. Bed, now, all of you." She gave Emot and Kai a look that said no arguing, and they all stood.

"Good night, sugar." Kai pressed a kiss to my lips and then walked off, followed by Emot doing the same.

"Sweet dreams, Maisie," Zugo said shyly, and closed his door leaving me alone with Sic, Cobra, and Viper.

"I will stay in the sitting room. In case you need anything, all you need to do is call out," Cobra said before looking at Sic. "Do not keep her up too long." Viper and Cobra walked out, closing the double doors as they went.

Sic slid up the bed further and grabbed my hand. "I really am sorry about earlier. I shouldn't have flown off the handle like that." He paused and pulled the covers up higher around me. "We've watched over you for so long, the idea that you might not want us, never crossed my mind. I should have realized that you didn't know us the way we knew you, and it's unfair of me to expect you to love us instantly." He turned to face the side doors while leaning his elbows on his knees.

"It isn't you, Sic. This whole situation is new, and I wanted to fight it, but I realized I can't." I slid out of the covers and put my hand on his arm drawing his attention to me. "I like you, all of you. I just didn't want a piece of paper, I had nothing to do with, to dictate my life. I still don't. It's not fair to the four of you or me." His face fell at my words, before I continued, "But I'm willing to ignore the paper and just get to know you and see where things go." His head lifted and his eyes locked on mine, I could see the hope under everything.

"I'm good with that, to just let things run their course however they will. You really should get some sleep, hopefully, you will feel better in a few days and we can talk more then." He rose and began to walk towards his own room.

"Sic, can I ask you something?" I paused as he turned back towards me and smiled.

"Anything. If it is in my power to give, I will," He said, and I felt a small grain of hope spark to life in my chest.

"Would you be willing to go see if my mother is alive?" I asked softly, hastily adding, "I'll stay here if that makes you feel better, I just need to know what happened."

He nodded once. "Yes, I can go check, but what if she isn't alive?"

"I guess, then I'll have my answer either way. I just need to know," I said, picking at the sheet on my legs. "Good night, Sic."

"Good night, honey." He walked to his room and slowly closed the door, leaving me alone.

The main door opened, and Viper flipped the light switch, leaving me in darkness. "Good night, Your Majesty. Sweet dreams."

"Good night Yixe, night Yoxe," I said to her back, and she sighed. Laying down, I thought I heard her mumble something about killing the old coots, then the darkness lulled me to sleep.

The rash was finally starting to fade from my skin, and after two days in bed, I had so much energy I wanted to run. Zugo was better, as well, so we had planned on getting him fully settled. Sic gave him a tour of the grounds and castle, except the next floor which even I hadn't been to. Emot showed him around the kitchens and his herb and vegetable gardens. Kai guided him around the outer walls and the main courtyard where the barracks were located, and the guards practiced.

He asked tons of questions, some I hadn't even cared to know the answers to, and we got to walk in the sun. We introduced Zugo to Yaga and Ahxezo, and they welcomed him just as warmly as they had me. They also inquired after my health and I assured them that I was doing much better. After lunch, I left the others and went to search out Cobra and Viper. They had set up their cabin in an open field near the Nymph lake.

I knocked on the door and Cobra opened it with a smile. "It is nice to see you back up and about, Maisie."

"I wanted to thank you for everything, helping Zugo and me. Not just through our illness, but through everything." She waved me in and closed the door behind me. I noticed their table was covered with hundreds of tiny houses. "What is all this?" Viper was organizing them into groups as she looked up at me.

"Oh, you know, just preparing in case they are needed," Viper said nonchalantly, waving my question away.

"Would you like some tea?" Cobra asked, and I cringed slightly.

"As long as it isn't that nasty stuff, then yes." Cobra laughed and began to gather stuff together.

"I have Leatherleaf tea. It has an apple flavor. How does that sound?" Cobra pulled a box off the shelf and prepped a few cups with different teas.

"None for me, thanks," Viper said, and Cobra put the third cup away.

She added hot water to both cups and then handed me one. I looked at the tiny leaves floating on top and shrugged, before taking a sip. The flavor was, indeed, apple in nature but there was a tart undertone that I couldn't place. I sat at the table and looked over the tiny houses with interest. "Do they all have furniture in them?" I asked, as I notice a tiny table in one.

"Yes, they do, and if we need them, we can make them full sized in a matter of seconds, so, don't rattle them around." Viper moved them out of my reach and began placing them in boxes.

"They are cute. Why are you making them?" Cobra and Viper exchanged a look then Cobra nodded.

"Well, to be honest, Cobra had a vision, and we are preparing just in case it was true. No need to worry just yet," Viper explained, as I drank the tea.

"Ok, well, I just wanted to thank both of you again for all your help." I finished off the tea and rose. "I'll let you get back to your tiny houses. Let me know if you need anything." Cobra walked me to the door picking my cup up along the way.

"Thank you, Maisie, for letting us stay here." She looked into the cup and smiled softly. "Enjoy your afternoon." I waved as

I walked back up to the castle. Zugo was standing outside the gates when I arrived.

"It's amazing, isn't it," He said, as I turned to stand next to him.

"The view, or being free?" I asked, and gazed out at the open grounds at the base of the mountain. The open land in the central part of Lasina was beautiful. Flowers dotted the grass and I began to see tiny lights flickering at the edge of the woods.

"I think both, to be honest. This view is breathtaking, all the more so because I'm free," Zugo said, as he reached out to touch my hand. We stood there holding hands for a moment, both of us just watching the world.

"Do you know what those are?" I asked, as I pointed to the flickering lights.

"I think they are the wood Sprites. At least from what I remember of my childhood. We used to go sit with them when I was young, my mother would talk with them." He turned and looked at me as he spoke. The silence not awkward but the air was charged. "You really are beautiful, Maisie."

I felt myself blush and smiled at his compliment, not really knowing how to respond. "May I..." he stalled and shook his head.

"What? You can ask me anything." I tried to get him to say what he wanted to.

"May I kiss you?" I chuckled softly at his polite request and yet, it was sweet. He was the first person to ever ask me for a kiss.

I turned towards him and rose onto my tip toes. "Anytime you want," I whispered, and pressed my lips gently to his. This

was a first for him, so I didn't go too fast or try to deepen it, just let him lead. His arms wrapped around me tightly, our fingers on one hand still locked together. When he stepped back, I sighed, and his eyes were glazed slightly.

"Thank you," he whispered, and then dropped my hand. "I should go, I told Sic I would help him get ready to go check on your mother." I watched as he turned and rushed back into the castle. My heart stuttered in my chest and I knew his sweetness would be my undoing.

I turned to walk back into the castle after Zugo, just as a tingle traveled up my spine, My body suddenly on fire for more contact. Kai saw me as I walked across the yard and I veered in his direction. Grabbing his hand, I pulled him along with me. He followed willingly until we got just inside the doorway then pulled me to a stop. "What's wrong?"

I honestly didn't know but I needed him, and immediately. "Where can we go? Some place private." He seemed to understand my request and picked me up making me squeak in shock. His footsteps were fast as he headed down a hallway, I hadn't paid attention to. Swinging a small door open, he placed my feet on the floor, in what looked like a small office.

"Is this private enough?" He asked, but I didn't answer, just grabbed his head and pulled him down for a kiss.

The small spark turned into an inferno and I began tugging at the button of his pants. He seemed to get the gist of what was happening and pulled his shirt off over his head before working mine off as well, our lips only breaking apart as he removed the fabrics. "Maisie, slow down, what's going on?" I got his pants unzipped and pushed them down his hips. His cocks sprung free as I dropped to my knees.

My answer was to wrap both hands around his cocks and lick both heads at once. "Fuck, Maisie." His hand tangled in my hair as I began to suck first one cock then the other, going back and forth. "Sugar, stop." I pulled his cock free and looked up his body, his blue eyes looked stormy with need.

"One," I said as I stood, and I watched his cocks shift into one then pulled my own pants off my hips. The sound of them hitting the floor snapped Kai into action and he picked me up as he kicked his own pants free. The blunt head of his cock rubbed my aching clit as he held me positioned over him.

He bit his lip and growled, "Say it, I can't until you say it."

"Fuck me, Kai," I whispered, as I pulled his lips to mine and he slid me down his length. He hissed as I cried out in pleasure and then began lifting me up and down his shaft. He

slowly backed up until he was able to sit on the edge of the table, then pulled my legs astride his hips and let me take over.

Riding his cock sent spikes of pleasure over my skin, his hands on my ass helped me rise and fall. "Gods, you look so sexy," He said as he captured my nipple in his teeth and hissed, "You're so tight." He leaned back pulling me down with him the table creaking as he began to thrust up into me.

"Kai, I need more," I begged, and he sat back up slightly and pulled me up off his cock. I almost cried at the loss until he flipped me over and then slid me back down facing away from him. The change in angle sent me higher as his finger circled my clit fast and hard. My orgasm raced along my veins and I screamed out as he pumped his hips faster.

As I came back down, Kai stood and turned so I was bent over the table. "Hold on tight," He said, as my feet slowly lowered to the floor. Griping onto the far side of the table tightly, Kai lifted my hips slightly and began to slam into me. Each thrust hard and fast, the more he gave me, the more I craved.

My cries grew louder with each thrust until the pleasure became overwhelming and I screamed as I flooded his cock and my thighs. I felt my pussy clamp down around his cock as he was held deep, his own roar of completion mixing with mine. My breath fogged the tabletop as I tried to slow my breathing, his hard cock still buried to the base.

I felt my body relax around him and he slid out slowly, helping me to stand. He spun me around and kissed me gently before picking me up once more. His hard cock was pressed between us and I realized he had only cum once. "I love when you cum on my cock," He whispered, as he walked me towards a couch I hadn't noticed before.

He laid me down on the soft cushions before covering my body with his. "Want more?" His question was soft and hopeful. I reached between our bodies and positioned him at my entrance, and he slid slowly in.

He didn't rush this time but drew out each movement for an eternity. "I love you, Maisie. I have for a very long time." I felt my heart ache with his words, but he didn't give me a chance to respond. Capturing my lips, he made love to my body and my mouth. The beauty of it, coming from Kai of all people, had tears gathering in my eyes. I could see Emot and Sic both making love, but Kai was unexpectedly tender.

My basilisk hissed her own pleasure but stayed buried, knowing instinctively I wasn't ready for a second mate. I could feel his weight pushing me into the cushions below us, but it was anything but uncomfortable. His arms were by my head as he stroked my hair and I felt a tear slip out. He lifted up and gazed at me. "Please don't cry, sugar." His thumb rubbed my tear away and I realized more were falling.

He stopped moving but didn't pull out. "Tell me what's wrong."

"Nothing is wrong... I just didn't expect this from you." He smiled and rolled his hips just a touch.

"You mean you expected nothing but hard and fast." He wiped my tears away and began kissing my face. "I am capable of taking things seriously sometimes, and you deserve to have both, the fast and the slow. Don't get me wrong, I love fucking, but this is nice, too." He began to move again, rolling his hips to press more along my g-spot.

"Kai, I don't know..." He stopped my words with a fierce kiss before breaking off.

41

"You don't have to say anything." He lifted my outer leg and held it by his hip as he rolled more. My body steadily climbing towards that sweet release I knew was coming. "Cum for me, sugar, I love feeling you cum around my cock," He spoke as he kissed my neck, working his way towards my ear. His tongue licked my lobe and then he nipped gently. My body tightened as he drove me steadily upwards, each stroke teasing the nerves in my body.

He recaptured my mouth as he increased his pace ever so slightly, and I felt my body start to spasm. The flood of release made his movements quicker and then I moaned into his mouth as I came apart. He groaned his own orgasm, as my body locked him tightly in place. We kissed for several minutes until my body began to relax and he slipped free, and placed his head on my chest. My fingers tangled in his hair as we both began to doze off in the warmth of our embrace.

Kai moving off me woke me up. I stretched as he picked up his clothes and then I noticed Emot standing by the doorway. He smiled at me as he picked up my shirt and pants, helping me dress. "Sssic isss leaving sssoon, to go check to see if your mother isss alive. He thought you might like to come sssay goodbye," Emot whispered, as he pulled my shirt over my head. "He'sss gonna be ssso mad when he findsss out you two were in hisss office," Emot teased, as I pulled my pants up.

"It was private," Kai said, as he pulled his shirt on and buttoned his pants.

"I don't disssagree, but if he findsss out..." Emot let his words trail off and grasped my hand. He kissed the back as we walked out the door. "Just don't tell him."

Laughing as we rounded the corner, I saw Sic standing at the top of the stairs. He looked frustrated, as if he had been searching for us. "There you are. I was hoping to get to see you before we left. Zugo is going to go with me and we are going to pack up anything that you might want. If your mother is alive, we will bring her back with us." He left the rest unsaid, knowing that the likelihood of her being alive was slim.

I followed Sic into the sitting room and Zugo smiled from the window seat before Sic pulled me away from Emot, into the bedroom. Closing the door, he pulled me closer hesitant about hugging me. "I know we still have ways to go to build our relationship..." He trailed off as I pressed a kiss to his lips.

"We have plenty of time," I said, wrapping my arms around his waist. "Thank you for checking on my mother."

"My pleasure, but if for some reason your mother is... dead. I need to know what you want me to do," His words were hesitant, like he didn't want me to have to think about that very real possibility. His arms wrapped around me, loosely returning my hug.

"I guess, bring her body back here for a burial." I closed my eyes hoping she was alright, but not daring to hope too much.

"I can do that." Sic tipped my chin up and his emerald eyes darkened with worry. "Be safe while I'm gone." He pressed his lips to mine and I began to feel sparks shiver along my nerves, but I pushed them down.

He stepped back and I let him go. Opening the door, he nodded to Zugo and then spoke to Emot and Kai., "You two, keep her safe. Are you ready to go, Zugo?"

"Yes." Zugo jumped up excitedly, going to Earth for the first time.

"Be safe, you two," Emot said, as Sic began to form a portal in the wall. I watched from the doorway as a blurry image of my bedroom appeared. Sic and Zugo stepped through the portal and it slid closed behind them.

"Well, what should the three of us do while we wait for them to return?" Kai asked, a devious smile on his face. Emot eyed him and then me before they both began to stalk closer, inching me backwards towards the bed. I couldn't help my scream as I began to run around the bedroom, both of them slowly closing in on me.

Kai and Emot stalked me from both sides of the bed as I stood in the center. I waited for them to lunge, then ran to the end, laughing as they missed me. I jumped off the bed and ran for the doors, kind of hoping they would catch me. When I threw the double doors wide, a startled guard dropped the hand he was about to knock with.

"Your Majesties." He bowed as the guys each flanked a side of me.

"Azeq, what are you doing here?" Emot asked, and paled. "Isss something wrong with my mother and father?"

Azeq, the guard looked up at Emot and gulped. "Your family is well, Your Majesty. However, your people are not. The Northern Kingdom attacked the border villages and people are fleeing to the capital. Your parents have no place for all the new arrivals and have asked us to seek out refuge for them."

Emot looked at me and all I could do was nod, then I remembered the tiny houses Cobra and Viper had been building. "Send them here, we shall house them until we take care of the Northern King," I spoke diplomatically, and he nodded and ran off.

"I suspect they will be arriving by nightfall. How will we protect them and house them all?" Kai asked me, as I closed the door.

"I think our game will have to wait a bit. We need to go see Cobra and Viper. Now, if possible." Kai pouted playfully and Emot pushed him away.

"Let'sss go," Emot spoke, as he walked towards the closet. "Sssince you will be meeting the Eastern Kingdom'sss sssubjects for the firssst time..." He trailed off as he reached into a safe on the wall. "You need to look the part of the Queen. Not to mention my parentsss will be helping." He held a large velvet box and placed it on the bed.

Kai walked into the closet and pulled a beautiful mint green dress off the rack in the back and brought it to me. "I don't really need to wear that do I?" I asked, as he laid the dress on the bed beside the velvet box. Emot opened it and the most beautiful tiara laid on the cushion inside. Mint green jewels highlighted rose gold filigree, and I ran my finger lovingly across the cool metal.

"It wasss your mothersss. Ssshe gave it to usss after we ssssigned the treaty," Emot whispered, as Kai began to undress me.

"Let's get you looking like a queen, even if for just a few hours." I balanced my hand on Kai's shoulder as he pulled my pants off my legs one by one. He slid his hand up my body as he stood, and I shivered.

"Don't ssstart Kai, we don't have time," Emot spoke, as he helped me step into the dress.

Once I was dressed, a knock sounded on the door and I saw Sage standing there. "Your Majesty, Viper told me to come

see if you needed any assistance in getting dressed." Her curiosity written on her face.

"Sssage, thank you. Will you help Maisssie put her hair up and sssecure this?" Her eyes widened as Emot held up the tiara, but she nodded, and we walked into the bathroom. Just as Sage started to close the door, Emot called out, "We will get ready and meet you out here when you're finissshed."

Sage closed the door and held the tiara reverently, afraid to move. "If you're afraid to hold it, how do you think I feel? I have to wear it." Sage laughed at my words, while placing the tiara on the vanity. I sat down and she began pulling my hair up into an intricate style. Letting curls fall down softly, she placed the tiara in firmly, and secured it with about a thousand bobby pins.

"There," She said, as she put the last one into my hair. "Wow, you look so much like your mother." I watched in the mirror as she dabbed her eye.

"Did you know my mother?" I asked, and she shook her head no.

"My mother grew up with Clara for a while. They were really good friends and she used to show me pictures of your mother. The one from your mother's wedding day was beautiful. she was wearing this very tiara and her jewels matched." Sage smiled as she opened the door. "Oh, my," She gasped, making me rise and turn towards the bedroom.

Kai and Emot stood dressed handsomely in what looked like ceremonial outfits, only differing in color. Emot's was black with lavender trim, while Kai's had red trim on a dark grey base. They both had a series of pins on their chest and both had rose gold braiding from their right shoulder to halfway down their chests. Kai's strained as his muscles flexed but Emot's fit perfectly.

"I think I need a bigger suit," Kai said, trying to loosen his shoulders some. "I hate this thing."

I joined them in the bedroom and ran my hand down both their chests appreciatively. "You two look so handsome." Sage nodded her agreement as I looked them over.

"They do, Your Majesty, and once you become the Empress, we can design them new ceremonial dress suits, so they all match. These are from their home countries," Sage commented, as she fixed one last curl in my hair. "You look beautiful, too," She whispered as she walked towards the doors.

"You do look magnificent, Maisssie," Emot said, as he held out his arm for me, Placing mine on his sleeve. Kai took my other hand, covering it with his own, and we walked out of the room. I desperately wanted to turn around and rip those clothes off them, but I would have to wait. The guards bowed as we walked down the stairs and then through the castle's main doors. Yaga and Ahxezo met us by the main gates as Cobra and Viper walked up the path.

"Your Majesties. We have been told of the situation and all is ready for expanding the castle's main battlements to encompass the valley, the Sprites have been appraised of our actions and approve of your determination to help those in need. They have agreed to allow the walls to surround their woods as well, with the understanding that nothing should be removed," Yaga practically yelled.

"We have also notified the Nymphs and they are perfectly happy with their lake being within the castle grounds, as long as they remain hidden from the general population. Yixe and Yoxe have prepared all the necessary buildings and are ready to begin once you give your final approval. They would also like Your Majesties to choose a new name for the town and help with the

placement of each home," Ahxezo continued where Yaga left off, and handed me a small wall looking structure. "If Your Majesty would place the first wall, we may begin."

I looked at Emot and Kai then my desperate gaze flew to Cobra's. She tilted her head off to the side and followed me as I walked to the corner of the current wall. "Here will do," She whispered, and I placed the tiny toy on the ground.

Emot and Kai stayed by my side as Cobra held out her arms and chanted a few words. The tiny wall instantly knitted itself into the existing wall, growing larger and longer, as it snaked its way around the entire mountain pasture and the woods and valley below. "Well fuck me, next time we build a nest, I'm calling Cobra," Kai said, and she threw him a glare. Massive gates and other entry points joined the wall, as it connected to the other side of the castle.

"Is Indra's pool included in the new walls?" I asked, and a section of the wall moved back a hundred feet further into the mountains.

"It is now," Viper said, as she handed me and the guys boxes filled with tiny houses. "We need to start placing these in the valley below." She didn't wait for an answer, just began walking down the path to an open area now surrounded by massive stone walls.

Cobra followed us down the path and as soon as we began lining up tiny houses in rows, she made them full sized. Rows became streets and soon an entire village was spread around us in the once open valley. Just as soon as the last house was full sized, the sound of people could be heard on the other side of the wall.

"They are here, Maisssie," Emot spoke beside me, as we walked towards the large gates. Guards were helping people with

injuries, as Cobra and Viper began guiding people to their new homes. They had left a large square open in the center for a marketplace and said we could work on paving it later.

"Have you figured out a name for this new town, Your Majesty?" Ahxezo asked, as he stepped up beside Emot and I. Kai joined us just as a large carriage rolled through the gate.

"Stormshade, I guess. What do you think?" Emot smiled at my suggestion, and we walked back up towards the castle gates to await his parents.

"I like it," Kai said, so Yaga announced the name to the people gathered around. Guards gathered around the new wall and cheered, while Yaga and Ahxezo directed people to their new homes. We reached the courtyard just as Emot's parents stepped down from their carriage.

"Emot!" A woman gleefully yelled, and ran to hug him. "I have missed you so much," She punctuated her words with motherly kisses, and he cringed.

"Mom, please ssstop." Emot tried to get out of her grip but she wouldn't let go.

"I haven't seen my baby in months; your father wouldn't let me come last time he was here. So, introduce me." She looped her hand through his arm and pulled him towards me. I knew by the look on her face that I was going to instantly like her.

"Mother, this isss Queen Margaret Day, Massisie this isss my mother, Essscu Howe, Queen mother of the Eastern Kingdom." Her eyes locked on Emot's and he smiled.

"Are you saying that you two have consummated the marriage?" She whispered, and I blushed bright red as Evat walked up to us.

"Now Escu, don't pry into your son's sex life. Your Majesty." He bowed to me and placed a kiss on my hand. "Please tell me I'm not the King anymore, I'm so ready to retire." His hardy laugh filled the courtyard as Emot pulled me to his side.

"Why don't we take this conversation inside?" Kai said, as he held out his arm to Escu, escorting her like a gentleman.

"It is wonderful to see you again, Margaret," Evat spoke, as he held out his own arm.

"You as well, Your Majesty," I said, and he frowned.

"Please, tell me I can retire," He whispered, and then laughed as we walked into the great hall. Emot had several of the staff get food and drinks while we sat around the table.

Emot sat next to his mom and Kai while I sat next to Evat. "I think you should remain in charge to some extent, until the treaty has been fully executed, but not as strenuously as before." He smiled as I spoke, the staff placing wine and snacks on the table for everyone.

"Your Majesty, the kitchens would like to know what they can do to help the people settle into their new homes," One of the head servers asked me politely.

"Do we have enough food to help families with meals?" I asked looking at Emot, and he nodded yes. "Why don't we prepare baskets for those who need things and distribute them around the village." The server grinned and ran off.

"So, Emot, answer my question, have you two made things official?" Escu asked, as the room fell silent and Kai snorted as Emot's face turned red.

"She wants to know if her baby boy has done the serpent slide, the reptilian rhumba, the tail twist, the snakey shakey, the cloaca coil, the basilisk boogie, the..." Emot smacked Kai as he laughed harder, cutting off his sentence. My own face turned red as Emot's dad started laughing, too.

"I think, it's safe to say they have," Evat said, as Kai fell out of his chair, he was laughing so hard.

"Oh, Kai, you want to tell them about your own afternoon activitiesss?" Emot said loudly over Kai's howls of laughter. Kai's laughter died quickly, just as Emot was about to tell his parents about the state he had found us in that afternoon.

"Can we please change the subject?" I said, before Emot could start in on his story. The night progressed more peacefully after that and, before too long, Emot's parents were saying their goodbyes.

"We will send more supplies for the village, until everyone is settled. We also let your father know what was going on, Kai, I am sure he will be sending things as well," Escu said, as we walked them towards the main doors. "It was so nice to meet you, Margaret." She pulled me in for a tight hug and I instantly missed my own mother, wondering how Sic and Zugo were doing.

"It was nice to meet you, as well, and thank you for your help," I replied, as she climbed up into the carriage. We stood on the steps leading into the castle and waved as they rolled away.

Kai swept me up into his arms and carried me inside and up the stairs. "Let's get you out of this dress and see if the three of

us can get tangled in the sheets." Emot walked up next to Kai and shook his head but I could see his smirk of agreement.

Zugo

The portal closed behind us and we stood in a silent house in an empty room. I noticed streaks of blood on the far wall, as Sic checked the hallway. "Let's go. The trail leads this way." Sic waved me on and I followed his footsteps warily. Pictures of Maisie lined the hallway walls, some from when she was a young child, others as a teen.

I gazed at the pictures as we walked slowly down the hall towards another bedroom. Sic paused at the door and slowly turned the knob, checking to see if the coast was clear. As he opened it wider, I noticed a large master bedroom that was torn to shreds. Fabric hung at odd angles on the windows and glass littered the floor. "Zugo, check the bathroom and closet. He began to search through the mess in the room as I opened the door.

There was blood on the mirror, and I could see a human foot lying in the open closet door. "Sic, in here." Sic dropped something on the floor and rushed by me. He flipped a light switch in the closet and dropped to his knees.

I watched as he felt the woman's neck and then called out, "She has a pulse, hand me that towel." I handed him the fabric he pointed at, and then knelt next to him. "She can't be moved. she wouldn't make it back to Lasina. If I make a portal to the castle,

would you bring Cobra and Viper back? They are the easiest to get, and my mother wouldn't be able to help this."

"Can you portal straight to Cobra and Viper, or will I need to find them?" I asked, as he assessed Maisie's mom. "And what should I tell Maisie if I see her."

"I'll make the portal to your room and you can bring Cobra, Viper and Maisie. She will need to be here," I heard a soft moan as Sic spoke. He looked down and spoke softly. "She's coming, Clara. We are getting help, just hold on." He made a portal behind me in the bathroom and I rose. "Hurry." He turned back to Clara as I stepped through.

Once back in my room, I noticed the clock on the wall, and it was late. I opened my door and got an eye full, as Maisie was sandwiched between Emot and Kai. I stood frozen for a moment and then Kai saw me standing there. "Fuck, man, you look like you saw a banshee." He stopped and Maisie looked over at me. Her cheeks were flushed, and I knew I looked like an idiot staring at her naked body.

"Zugo, are you alright?" she said as she climbed off Emot, and then my brain snapped back into motion.

"I need to get Cobra and Viper, and we need to go back," I said, and she paled.

Kai picked Maisie up and set her on the floor. "Get dressed." She ran to the closet and I began walking to the doors. I flung them open and saw Cobra and Viper standing there, patiently waiting with bags in hand.

"Hurry up, Maisie!" Viper yelled, as Kai and Emot scrambled into their clothes.

Maisie ran out of the closet, still pulling a shirt over her head, then we were all walking to my room. The portal still glowed as Cobra and Viper held hands and stepped through, followed by Kai. Emot went next as Maisie hesitated. "Tell me Zugo, is she... is she dead?"

I couldn't help it, I pulled her in for a tight hug as I spoke, "No, but I don't think she has long." She forced herself to take a deep breath and stepped through.

As soon as I followed her, the portal closed, and Kai was holding Maisie upright as she took in the scene in the bathroom. Cobra and Viper were swiftly working to save Clara while Maisie watched, Kai holding her upright. Sic had been pushed back out of the way and he stood with Emot. "Mais..." Clara's voice was barely audible, and Maisie instantly crawled into the closet with Cobra and Viper.

Maisie grabbed Clara's hand and whispered, "I'm here Mom, we're gonna get you fixed up."

"Maisie, be happy," Clara tried to speak, but only mumbles came out. Sic whispered to Emot and Kai. They left the room, I could hear what sounded like large objects being moved. When I looked over my shoulder, I saw that they were packing Clara's things into a tiny bag much like Cobra had when she moved the cabin.

I watched as Cobra tried to heal Clara, but it didn't do any good. "She's too far gone Maisie. I can't heal her." Maisie sobbed and Clara's hand reached up to cup her cheek.

"Mom, you can't leave, you have to fight," Maisie pleaded, as tears ran down her face. I knew the pain she was going through, and as much as I wanted to take it away, I couldn't.

"Be a... kind ruler, a smart... ruler, a just... ruler, and a... loving ruler. I am so... proud of you... Maisie. I love you," Clara's words were broken and hushed, but she eventually got them out making Maisie cry harder.

Maisie put her head on Clara's chest as Clara stroked her hair, and then her hand slid off Maisie's head, and I knew she was gone. Maisie bawled as she held her mother's body, and I felt my own tears trailing down my cheeks. Cobra tried to pull Maisie away, but she wouldn't budge, so she and Viper left the closet.

"Give her a few minutes, we will go pack the rest of the house, and then we need to take her back. We can bury Clara in Lasina," Viper whispered to Sic, and he nodded his understanding.

Several minutes passed before Sic helped Maisie stand, picking her up when her legs gave way beneath her. He cradled her to his chest, as the others returned. "Kai, please bring Clara so we can give her a proper burial back home." Kai handed his bag to Emot, and gingerly lifted Clara's body.

Sic created a portal to the castle, and we filed through, Kai last. The great hall was silent as Kai laid Clara on the table, and a servant brought out a white sheet. They covered all but her face and Cobra placed a hand on Clara's forehead. "We shall stay with her tonight, and get her cleaned up before we let the people know."

"Thank you, we will make arrangements for the people to be able to see her and say goodbyes," Sic said, Maisie still crying in his arms.

He carried her up the stairs and when I went to follow, Kai placed a hand on my arm. "Give them some time." I watched as they disappeared out of sight, and then Emot and Kai pulled me

towards the outer yard, and towards an outbuilding. Two older men stood out front, tears in their eyes as they gazed towards the castle.

Maisie

Sic carried me into our sitting room and sat by the fire on the floor. He didn't say anything, just let me cry out my grief on his shoulder. His hand rubbed my back soothingly until my tears slowed and eventually stopped. When I lifted my head, his shirt was soaked. "I'm sorry," I whispered, pulling the shirt off his skin.

"Don't apologize, you just lost your mother, and a wet shirt won't kill me." He continued to rub my back as I laid my head back on a dry spot.

He slid back from the fire, so his back rested on the couch, and shifted me into a more comfortable position. "We need to plan a ceremony for your mother. If you don't feel up to it, the guys and I can take care of it," His words were gentle, as he cradled me in his lap.

"What needs to happen?" I asked, not knowing all that needed to be done.

"We will plan a day for the people to pay tribute to your mother. She will be in the great hall. Then, there will be burial, and a monument erected in her honor. We will see if the Nymphs will allow us to bury her in their valley, so she is nearby. Kai will be able to help plan, his mother passed last year, and the service was beautiful. My dad died a few years back, but it's a bit different

for born Kings. There is more pomp and ceremony involved in a King's death. But we can do anything you want," He explained, trying not to overwhelm me, but the idea of planning was so foreign to me that I didn't think I could do it.

"I don't know, maybe I'll just let you guys take care of it," My whisper was soft, and he hugged me tighter as the tear threatened again. "Please talk about something else. I don't want to cry anymore."

"Kai's a pain in the ass," He said, and a watery laugh crossed my lips. "He was making cum puns earlier."

"He was also making jokes about sex when Emot's parents were here," I sighed, as I remembered the embarrassment.

"I do need to discuss something with you, but I hesitate to bring it up right now," Sic's words seemed ominous, and his face was pained when I looked up at him.

"Just rip the band aid off, and tell me," I said, sitting up more so I could see him fully.

Sic cupped my cheek and wiped his thumb across it. "I know I'm not the easiest person to get along with, and I need to remember that I've had a lot longer to get used to this than you have. I've been thinking a lot about it and I'm more than willing to step down, and let my brother take my place, if that's what you want," His words were a shock, and I scrambled off his lap. My basilisk hissed her anger at his words, and I had to seriously focus on not shifting.

I could see the scales pressing to the surface of my skin mirrored by Sic's own. "How could you say that? Even after everything I don't want someone else." He stood up towering over me, and I looked up at his face. He seemed relieved, and yet still torn.

"You know that it doesn't have to be me, I have a brother who is about Zugo's age," He pressed on, and I pulled him closer, my hands fisted in his shirt.

"Hear my words and truly listen. I. DON'T. WANT. ANYONE. ELSE. Excluding Kai, Emot and Zugo. I don't want your brother. my basilisk doesn't want anyone else. So, get that idea out of your head." I loosened my grip on his clothes as he stepped closer. "No one can replace you Sic, despite the work we need to do to get to a point of understanding. You just pulled away when I didn't choose you first, and I don't see what the big deal is with the order. So, you weren't the first, that doesn't mean you're a never." He stopped whatever else I might have said when his lips pressed to mine.

He pulled me against his chest tightly and I opened for him to deepen the kiss. I wrapped my hands around his neck as he picked me back up and cradled me in his arms once more. Sitting on the couch, he broke the kiss and pressed his forehead to mine. "I have loved you for a while now, and it never occurred to me that you might not feel the same way. I just wanted you to have options if this wasn't what you wanted."

"None of this is what I wanted, but I realized, it might just be what I needed, and I want it now. I want you just as much as them." I laid my hand over his heart feeling its stead beat, my head, I rested back on his shoulder. We sat in silence like that, just enjoying the peace. I knew things would be rocky and we would need to work together to succeed, but I was willing to try if he was.

A soft knock on the door had Sic turning his head. "Can I come in?" Zugo's head peeked around the doorway.

"Sure," Sic said, and I watched Emot and Kai sneak by and head into the bedroom, while Zugo came and sat by the fire. He didn't say anything at first, and we just sat in a peaceful silence for a while. My eyes zoned out as I watched the flames dance in the fireplace. Sic rose and I clung to his shirt, worried that he would leave, as he placed me on the couch. "I'm going to shower and change." He slid his thumb across my lower lip before standing upright. "I'll be back in a bit."

He walked to the bedroom, leaving Zugo and I alone. Zugo stood and sat on the couch next to me. "I'm sorry about your mother. is there anything I can do? Kill someone, maim someone, fuck someone?" He laughed at the last part and so did I.

"Kai is rubbing off on you," I chided softly.

"Is that such a bad thing?" He asked as he slid close, nervously putting an arm around me.

"Not necessarily, but I like you the way you are." I cuddled closer letting him know without words that he could hold me.

"You like a bitter virgin who has been locked up most of his life and just wants to kill the man who locked him up? Somehow, I doubt that," He said seriously, but with a hint of sarcasm in his voice.

"I understand the desire you have to get revenge, but I think you are better than that. And if it comes down to it, you wouldn't kill for revenge but to save innocent people," I spoke, and he shrugged.

"You're probably right, but can I still let Kai corrupt me? He's fun to hang with," He asked, and I laughed.

"I guess, just don't let him rub off on you too much," I giggled at my slight joke, and he smiled until we noticed Viper standing in the doorway.

"Do you think you could get the others and come down to the great hall, we found something you all need to see," Her words made me forget about the teasing between Zugo and I. Rising, I nodded and walked into the bedroom.

Kai's door was open and Emot was standing shirtless in the doorway, talking with Kai. Sic's door was closed, so I walked to Kai's room first, Emot pulling me in for a hug as I stopped next to him. "Viper found something and needs us in the great hall." Kai rose from his bed as I turned to go get Sic.

Emot and Kai walked past me into the sitting area as I knocked on Sic's bedroom door. There wasn't an answer, so I slowly opened the door. The sound of the shower could be heard from the door, so I walked to the bathroom entryway. Sic stood in the water facing the wall, I could see his full back and ass. A thin scar ran around the side of his hip and spider webbed up his back, and I wondered how I hadn't noticed it before.

He lifted his head up and caught sight of me in the mirror before turning around. His hand reached for the handle to turn the water off as he grabbed his towel off the hook with the other. Stepping out of the shower, he wrapped it around his hips and then asked. "What's wrong?"

I wet my, suddenly dry, lips with a quick dart of my tongue and answered his question, "Viper said they found something and need to see us."

"I'll be right there." He pulled the towel off his hips and began drying off, and I tried my damnedest not to drool. The sight of his muscles flexing had me suddenly wanting to forget this whole night and just explore his body.

He noticed me still standing there and smiled. Then he walked towards me, dropping the towel. His hand snaked out and grabbed my wrist, and then he pulled me to his room. "Go, I'll be right behind you." He slapped my ass playfully and then began to dress as I walked out.

Viper was standing by the bedroom door tapping her foot impatiently. "Hurry up, this isn't the time to be ogling the goodies." I blushed as she pushed me towards the sitting room doors. "Sic, get your ass out here!" She yelled, as I neared the others. Once Sic walked out of the room, Viper pushed us all out and down stairs to the great hall.

When we entered the great hall, all the tables had been removed and the walls were draped in a dark green cloth. My mom's body was still laid on a table, but she looked peaceful, like she was sleeping. She was dressed in a dark green dress that made her blond hair look even lighter, and her lips looked redder. Cobra stepped forward and pulled two bags off a small side table and handed them to me. "This is everything that was in your home back on Earth, if you ever want to go through it." I smiled softly as she patted my hand.

"We found two things that shouldn't have been there. They have no trace of Clara on them. This was gripped in her fist," Viper said, and held up a small necklace that had an ouroboros pendant with a yellow gem for its eye.

"Why would she have a Jörmungandr pendant?" Kai asked, as if the necklace was one he had never seen before. "Clara never

66

wore anything reminiscent of Lasina; in fact, she made sure not to, in case someone noticed."

"Why does it look so familiar?" Sic asked Cobra, and she looked at him sharply.

I watched his face for a moment, but it didn't seem to register. Viper held up a shirt next, it was soaked in blood and torn in several places. "This was also near Clara when we cleaned up the closet."

"That's my shirt, but it was ruined when Kai was injured. Sic and I used it to slow his bleeding until Salima was able to get here. Why would my mother have it?" I took the stiff fabric and noticed that it had been shredded in spots.

Emot looked at the shirt and sniffed. "It smells like bird."

"That's what I thought as well, and wasn't the man who broke into the castle a bird shifter?" Viper asked, as Emot took the shirt from me.

"What if someone went back to my house after Vago got back here, and killed her?" I asked, and Cobra nodded once.

"That is my suspicion, she would not have survived that long with the injuries she had. The damage to Clara was done within a day or two. Someone went back to finish the job. I found several healing bruises that were most likely from when Vago attacked her, but he left her alive," Viper spoke to the guys, and then looked at me. "I think he may even still love your mother on some level. Because all she had were bruises. The injuries that killed her were different, precise and very thin. My guess is, a woman did it, and one that Clara knew."

"What should we do?" Kai asked them, as Emot handed the shirt back to Viper.

"Unfortunately, I can't see who did this. Something is blocking my vision, and for that to happen, they have to be very powerful. My suggestion would be to trust no one, until we know who has that power," Cobra spoke softly to the guys, then looked at me. "Trust your gut Maisie, it just might save your life," With that said, they said their goodbyes to us and to my mother, then walked towards the main doors. "Oh, and Maisie." I turned to see that Cobra had paused. "Everything will work out, I promise, just give it time."

Her words were cryptic as always, and I wondered what she was talking about. As they left, I walked over to my mother and picked up her lifeless hand. I heard Sic tell the others to give me a minute, and I heard them walk off as I said my own goodbyes to my mother. She looked so peaceful it was hard to imagine that her last moments were so terrible. I could feel Sic's presence behind me, and softly whispered, "I just can't believe she is gone. I know she is, but it doesn't feel real."

"I know, some days it doesn't feel real that my dad is gone, and he died a few years ago, just after my mom had my baby brother," Sic's voice was right behind me, and he wrapped his arms around me giving some comfort. "You should get some sleep. Tomorrow, we will plan her funeral and everything. Cobra put her in a frozen state until after the funeral, so people could say goodbye." He loosened his grip and I bent forward to kiss my mom's head, then we walked back up the stairs together.

Once we were back in the room, I noticed the other's doors were open as Sic helped me get ready for bed. He tucked me in and then sat on the edge. "We will leave the doors open if that's okay with you, just in case you need something." I nodded, and he rose to kiss my forehead before walking to his own room,

hitting the light switch as he went. The room darkened further as they turned their lights off and then I laid in the dark, strangely numb.

Two Days Later

The morning of the viewing arrived, and Sage came early to help me dress. I was required to wear a dark green dress which, she explained, was the mourning color here, and the tiara I wore the other day. She did my hair more formally than the other night, and whispered., "I am very sorry, Your Majesty, the whole of Lasina is. People have arrived from all over to pay their respects, and Thuzo has upped the guards ten-fold to protect you, and the new village."

I grabbed her hand and squeezed softly. "Thank you, Sage. I am so grateful to have you here."

"I am grateful you let me move in. Thuzo and I have set a date, but it is still a ways off." She smiled as I stood.

"Do I look alright?" I asked, and she nodded.

"You look perfect. Again, I am so sorry." I couldn't help but hug her tight to thank her, before walking out of the bathroom.

The guys were lined up wearing dark green suits, and I smiled at how nice they looked, despite the somber occasion. Sic came forward and offered me an arm so we could walk to the viewing. They told me that the public would have one day to say goodbye, and then the funeral would be the following day, privately. I knew Emot's parents were coming and Kai's dad, as well as Sic's mother, but that was it.

"Did you invite my father, by chance?" I asked Sic, as we walked down the stairs.

"Are you nuts? No. I'm not letting that man within a hundred yards of you, ever again," Sic's reply was hushed, but no less deadly serious.

"Did anyone notify him?" I asked. "I mean, at one point he had to have loved her, right? shouldn't he know?" I felt guilty that he wouldn't be able to say his respects to his own wife, even if he did try to kill her.

"Yes, an envoy was dispatched to inform him," He whispered, as we neared the bottom. "They returned with no information about his reaction, and they weren't let onto the North Kingdom lands." He stopped speaking as the doors in front of us were opened to a long line of people waiting to pay their respects. The guards parted and followed us to a dais where five throne-like chairs had been placed. Sic helped me sit in the middle one, and the others sat in the two on either side of me.

Guards lined the front of the dais as people slowly began to follow a line around my mother's body. Most kissed their hands and placed them on her forehead; some outright bawled, and a few knelt to pray. The day wore on as more and more mourners filed through the doors, until I recognized a family that entered the castle doors.

Indra and Wade were dressed finely and had both children with them. When they neared, Sic told the guards to let them pass, and Indra went down on one knee. "Your Majesty, I am deeply sorry for your loss, and the merpeople grieve for you, as well. As a tribute to your mother, the Merpeople shall not light the night sky for three days, in honor of your loss, and to show our own grief."

"Please rise, Indra. You do not need to bow here," Sic spoke, allowing Wade to help her rise. "It is very kind of the Merpeople to extend their heartfelt sympathies, and it is greatly appreciated."

Indra and Wade backed off the dais and returned to the line, saying their own farewells to my mother. They moved along with the line and then they were gone once more. The sky darkened as the last few mourners passed through the doors, and the line finally ended. Sic rose and knelt near my head. "There are only a few more, and they requested to come after everyone else had gone."

I looked up at him curiously and asked, "Who would wait until the very end?" As soon as I spoke, I saw the Nymph King and his son walk through the doors.

"Your Majesties, Maisie." The King stopped just outside of the guards and I rose along with the others. I noticed they both wore clothing in the same dark green as we did. "I am deeply grieved by your loss and wish to say that we shall watch over your mother's grave for as long as Nymphs reside in the lake." He grasped my hands and kissed both cheeks before allowing his son to do the same.

They both paid their respects to my mother, and before they left, they assured me that they were grateful for the wall and the protection. "The Sprites have agreed to decorate the

gravesite, and together, we will make sure your mother is well honored," the King spoke one final time, and they made their way back out again. Once the doors to the castle closed, I realized how exhausted I was.

"You did wonderfully Maisie, it is difficult, I know. Emot is going to get something for you to eat and bring it upstairs," Kai said, as he held out his arm, for once being serious. I yawned as we began walking back upstairs towards the room, and tomorrow looked to be another hard day.

The funeral was simple, and we gathered around the gravesite as the glass coffin was lowered into the ground. Emot's mother cried the entire time and so did Emot's dad. I remembered Evat saying he had once been betrothed to my mother, but I hadn't known that they had remained friends. After the service, I watched the tiny lights flutter out of the trees and cover the grave with beautiful flowers.

"Your Majesty, it is an honor to help in any way we can," A tiny Sprite piped up from in front of me, after the flowers began to bloom. "Your mother was an amazing woman." The Sprites left almost as quickly as they had arrived, leaving nothing but wildflowers in their wake.

Sic walked up next to me and placed a hand on my back. "Are you ready to go back?" I nodded and turned, noticing the others had begun the short hike to the castle. Salima waited for a moment until everyone was gone before approaching.

"Might I have a word with my son?" She asked politely, but Sic stiffened beside me.

74

"Anything you have to say, Mother, you can say in front of Maisie," Sic replied, not removing his hand from the small of my back.

Salima looked at me and glared slightly before focusing on Sic. "I want you to come home," She demanded as if he were still a child.

"What do you mean, come home?" He asked in disbelief.

"Forget this treaty and come home where it's safe," She pleaded, entirely ignoring my existence.

"It's a little late for that, Mother. The treaty has been signed," I could hear the frustration in Sic's voice, as she became more demanding.

"Then fuck her to make it valid and come home." She gestured in my direction and stomped her foot.

"Excuse me, this is my wife your talking about, despite the fact that the union isn't consummated yet, we are technically married," His voice became almost a deadly hiss, as he informed her of the facts. "Besides, you haven't given me a good enough reason to want to leave."

She pointed at me and then sneered, "Because everyone who gets near her is either injured or winds up dead. I don't want the next funeral to be yours." She faked a concerned look but didn't fool either Sic or me.

"Don't you think this motherly protection goes against your norm, Mother?" Sic spoke in a quiet whisper, and her face turned beet red in anger.

"No, Vago is actively hunting her and you could have been killed while trying to rescue her from his clutches," My brain snapped on her words, but I couldn't place what was off about them. Sic's hand left my back and he held out his arm to me.

"This conversation is over, Mother. we are going back to the castle for lunch." He placed my arm on his sleeve, and we began walking away.

"I can't protect you if you choose to ally yourself with her; please don't do this." Sic ignored her and we kept walking.

"Why would she say that?" I whispered, as we headed back.

"I have my suspicions but nothing definite yet, if that changes, I'll let you know," He spoke softly, as we turned up the path.

Emot, Kai, and Zugo were waiting for us at the top of the path when we arrived. "Everything alright?" Emot asked Sic, as we walked through the gates.

"Everything is fine. Let's go eat," Sic replied, as Emot walked beside us. I thought about it and realized I needed to give them some alone time soon.

Once we were inside, the servers set the table for everyone and had a small lunch prepared. Salima didn't join us and I wasn't the least bit sorry about it. Sic didn't seem surprised or sorry, either. Emot's parents and Kai's father told stories about my mother, just reminiscing about the past. It was nice to see a different side of her than I had before. They didn't stay long after lunch, and Escu made sure to hug me goodbye, while also mentioning her desire to visit soon.

We waved farewell from the gates as they all left, and then Kai scooped me up in his arms. "How does a nap sound, just the two of us?" I rolled my eyes, but it did sound kinda nice, so I let him carry me up to the bedroom.

11

Maisie

More victims of Vago's attacks arrived in the village and we added more houses as needed. The days were busy as we helped people get settled in. I was walking through the village with Zugo and Sic when Sic pulled me to a stop letting Zugo walk ahead a bit. "I wanted to ask if you would go on a date with me?"

"You don't have to ask me on a date? We spend time together every day," I replied, trying to laugh off his question.

"I know, but I mean just the two of us, like a real date," Sic clarified, looking oddly nervous.

I decided to tease him just a bit. "What did you have in mind?"

His steps faltered for a moment before he caught up with me. "Well, I was actually thinking about taking you to see the nesting grounds. You have met Indra, the Nymphs, and the Sprites already, but the Gryphons, while wild, are still friendly. They live deeper in the mountains to the South." He smiled as we began the walk up to the castle. "We can ride on the unicorns to get there." The girly girl in my heart squealed her delight at riding a unicorn.

Trying to control my excitement, I nodded. "I would like that." Realizing I really would like that, my excitement built more as we entered the castle. "When would you like to go?"

"I was thinking in half an hour. You can change into comfortable clothes, then we can leave. I'll get the unicorns ready to go. I think we can leave the guards here for this trip since we are only going into the mountains." Sic smiled as I did a giddy little dance and ran halfway up the stairs, before turning back.

"Will we be able to feed them, do you think? Oh, never mind." I squealed and raced up the rest of the stairs. The doors opened wide as I ran in, startling Kai and Emot. "No time to talk, unicorn rides and Gryphons," I yelled as I ran past, ripping off my dress before I even made it to the closet. While I was Rummaging around for comfy clothes, Kai walked into the doorway to watch me change.

"Jeans might be best," He commented, as I hopped into a pair of leggings almost falling over in the process. "Trust me, you want jeans, not leggings." Pulling the leggings off, I tossed them at Kai, as he handed me the jeans.

"Thank you," I mumbled, and pulled the jeans on as fast as possible. I grabbed the shoes and started for the door.

Kai's hand snaked out and grabbed my waist, and he pulled me to a stop by his side. "Forgetting something?"

"Oh." I stretched up and kissed him, but he didn't release me.

"As much as I appreciate the kiss, you might want a shirt too." Looking down, I realized I was still topless, and I laughed at myself.

"You are probably right." I ripped a shirt of a hanger and put it on as fast as I could, while still holding my shoes. "Thank you again." I kissed him once more and then rushed out of the closet. Stopping by Emot, I kissed him too, then ran out the door.

"Hey, what about my kiss?" Zugo's voice came from the top of the stairs as I passed. Pausing, I gave him a swift kiss before running down the stairs and outside. The unicorns were on the steps, saddled and ready to go, Sic was fastening a few bags to his saddle as I plopped down on the steps to put my shoes on.

Once my shoes were on, I jumped up. "I'm ready." Sic laughed softly, walking over to me.

"That took you all of ten minutes. I still need to get the stuff together, then we can go." He pulled me closer for a moment. "Why don't you go see if you can snag us some raw meat from the kitchens, then you can feed the Gryphons." He pushed me back towards the castle doors with a smile.

I rushed to the stairwell and slid down two stairs in my hurry before slowing enough so I wouldn't break my neck. The kitchen staff was busy making baskets for the new arrivals to the village. One of the head cooks noticed me standing there and walked over. "May I help you, Your Majesty?" He bowed low as he spoke.

"Please don't bow, and I was hoping to get some raw meat from you to feed to the Gryphons." He smiled and went to the large fridge, pulling two large paper packages out.

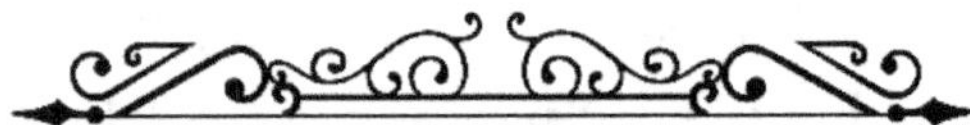

"His Majesty asked for me to prepare these for just that reason. Have a wonderful time," he said, handing over the meat, and I realized it was heavier than I had expected it to be.

"Thank you." Walking out of the kitchen and back up the stairs took longer than I thought, with as heavy as the meat was. Sic took it from me and loaded the second unicorn's saddlebags with the packages.

"Here, let me help you up." He placed his hands on my waist and lifted me up into the saddle, handing me the reins. He climbed up into his own saddle and then smiled. "Ready?" I grinned in glee, making him laugh as he urged his mount forward, mine following naturally after his.

We followed a rough trail through the mountains for about half an hour until we reached a beautiful mountain glade. The field was covered in tall grass and wildflowers, and I noticed a small golden lake on the far side. Sic pulled to a stop near some trees and hopped down. Tying his unicorn to a tree before helping me down and tying mine next to his. He grabbed the meat, as well as what he had packed in his saddle bags, handing me a blanket.

"I didn't bring any food because I figured we would go back before dinner, but this way, you can sit down and feed them. The babies should come right up to us and sitting helps them feel comfortable." He began to walk towards the woods, and I looked back at the field. "They live in the trees. this way."

We walked deeper into the cool darkness beneath the canopy of blue and pink leaves until we reached a small clearing. He placed the meat down and took the blanket from me before spreading it out. We sat down and he opened one of the packages

of meat and tossed several small chunks around us, and we waited.

It didn't take long before a large adult flew down from the trees and began picking at the meat that we had tossed out. "She is checking to make sure we are friendly. Gryphons are still animals, but highly intelligent and know a friend from a foe," Sic explained, as the gryphon tilted her head this and that way, while looking at us. She let out a loud screech and dozens more flew down from the trees. "If you hold out some meat, they will take it from you." He handed me several small pieces and held his own hand out.

A large Gryphon came in and gently took the meat from his hand, as several tiny Gryphons walked underneath the large one. I held my hand out lower and three babies raced towards my hand. They pecked the meat up swiftly and then squawked for more. Sic placed the package between us and I picked up more as the babies practically knocked me over to get to it. I laughed as bird claws and lions' paws crawled all over my lap. The large gryphon made a noise and all three backed off and sat.

They waited patiently for me to hand them each another piece and then more babies arrived. Before long, dozens of babies were all clamoring for a treat, while the adults watched from just behind them. Sic pulled the second package open and rose, feeding each of the adults while the babies chirped for more around me. I reached out and stroked baby beaks and feathers, as their tails flicked happily. Once all the meat was gone, the babies began to run around the clearing.

"We need to clean our hands, one sec." Sic pulled a water bottle from the bag he had and a hand sanitizer. Wetting a towel, we cleaned our hands and then sanitized before he put it all back. "So, what do you think?" Sic asked, as he sat back down.

I watched the babies romping around as the adults watched from the lower branches of the trees. "They are fantastic, and so well mannered." I laughed as two babies rolled around together in the grass. Sic reached over and tucked a loose hair behind my ear making me look over at him.

"I'm glad you're having a good time. I like to come here when I need alone time, but I thought you would enjoy it." He turned and looked out over the grove and I was struck by how handsome he was. They were all amazing to look at, but I hadn't really taken the time to truly look. He turned back to look at me and smiled, melting my heart that much more. "Is everything okay?"

"Yes, it's perfect," I said, while scooting closer to him.

"I didn't bring you out here to try to get into your pants, Maisie," He spoke, as I leaned against him.

"I know, but does that mean you wouldn't if given the chance," I asked before climbing into his lap, so I was facing him.

"I'm not a monk," He whispered just before my lips pressed his. I ran my tongue along his lips, and he deepened the kiss, sweeping into my mouth.

I broke the kiss after a moment and sighed. "Sic, do you think..." I trailed off and bit my lower lip.

"What? You don't have to hide anything. I mean, technically, we are married, at least on paper," He said, as he tipped my chin up. "What do you want?"

Nervously, I looked around and pushed him back onto the blanket. "Would you eat me like you did the other day?" He growled low in his throat and rolled us, so I was pinned below

him. His lips captured mine and I felt his fingers working my pants open. He pulled my jeans down my hips and then off, placing them next to me.

I began lifting my shirt, but he stopped my hands. "Not here," He whispered as he slid himself down my body, kissing my lower stomach and hip bones before blowing warm air on my core. His lips began kissing slowly until his tongue flicked out and ran along my slit. I arched up, as my hand tangled in his hair, and he swirled his tongue around my clit.

He sucked my clit as he held my hips pinned in place and then I felt his basilisk tongue slide deep into me. I moaned as he used his tongue much like a dildo and used the fork at the end to tease my g-spot. Back and forth, from my clit to my g-spot, had me practically thrashing my head in pleasure. My fist tightened in his hair as his hands slid up my thighs opening them wider, allowing him better access. He was relentless in his pursuit of my orgasm and it didn't take him long.

My back arched as I flooded his mouth and my pussy rapidly spasmed around his forked tongue. He slowly crawled up my body until his cocks rubbed me through his pants. Rolling his hips, he rubbed my clit, but never tried to take his clothes off. He was grinding on me hard, and my body was rising to a second peak. I cried out hearing his hiss of pleasure at the heat between my thighs. His lips pressed on mine before he whispered, "If we don't stop, I'm going to cum in my pants, and probably end up with claw marks on my back."

I opened my eyes to see Sic, and a second pair of eyes tilted curiously from his shoulder. A baby Gryphon had perched on Sic's shoulder at some point, while he was making me cum, and it sat there watching. I couldn't help but giggle at its curious face.

Sic slowly rose off me and the baby hopped down next to us. "This is why I said, 'not here' to your shirt." While he spoke, the baby poked at something on the ground, then ran off, my pants dragging behind it. "Shit."

Sic jumped up, as the baby ran around the clearing making soft squawks of triumph. Several other babies chased the one with my pants, as Sic ran after them. I sat up, not able to control my laughter as they began to fly off, in a game of keep away. They deliberately kept my pants away from Sic as they flew just out of his reach. All of a sudden, a loud screech filled the air around us and the babies dropped to the ground leaving the pants behind before flying off.

Sic picked up my pants and walked back to the blanket, shaking them out before handing them over. I slid them on, noticing several small holes from the Gryphons' tug of war. Once dressed, Sic picked up our trash and the blanket along with the small bag. He held my hand as we walked back to where the unicorns were tied up and he kissed me before helping me up. "Did you have a good time?" He asked, as I got settled into the saddle.

I bent forward and pressed my lips to his once more. "I did, thank you." He smiled as he untied my mount and handed me the reins. Within moments, his own was untied and we began riding back towards the castle trail. "Maybe when we get back, you and Emot can put on a show for me," My words were whispered so low, I almost hoped he didn't hear, but his eyes locked onto mine, and I knew he had.

He smiled a devilish smile and said in a decidedly sensual voice, "As my queen commands." The rest of the walk back was silent, but charged with a different type of tension, of a more pleasurable nature. The sun setting as we slowly made our way back.

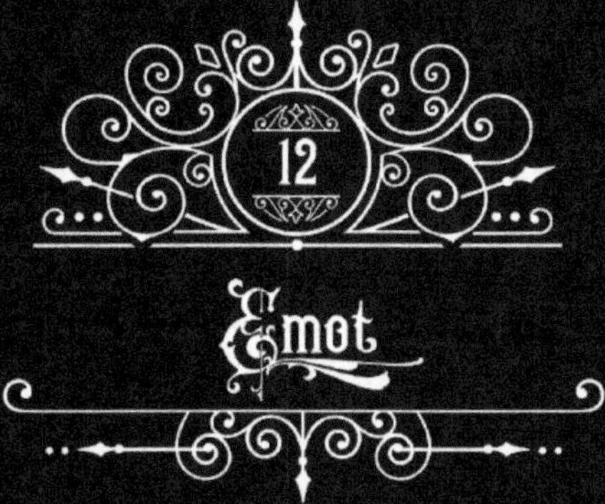

12

Emot

I watched Viper slink away from the castle into the night as Cobra walked up towards the castle. She saw me standing in the gateway, looking out over the village, waiting for Maisie to come back. "Where isss Viper off to?" I asked, as she stopped by my side.

"She is off to track a killer; she has an idea of who is behind Clara's death, and decided some recon was required," Her answer was somewhat expected considering it was Viper we were discussing. "Why are you standing out here in the dark?"

"Just waiting for Sssic and Maisssie to arrive back, I expected them back by now, but they are ssstill out." My eyes scanned the path into the mountains, looking for them once more. I saw the silhouette of two figures cresting the ridge and breathed a sigh of relief.

"There they are, and I suspect you will be a busy boy tonight." Cobra laughed as she patted my hand. "I am off to see Yaga and Ahxezo for a bit. Enjoy your evening." She walked away as Maisie and Sic rode closer and I enjoyed the view they made. I hadn't spent any time alone with Sic lately, and realized how much I had missed him these last few weeks. On the other hand, Maisie had become an obsession, my need for her driving me mad.

I walked back into the main courtyard as they passed through the gates and stopped near the stairs. The stable hand came out and took their reins, as Sic hopped down and helped Maisie off her unicorn. "How wasss the ride?" I asked, as they walked up the steps.

"It was amazing. The baby Gryphons are so adorable, even though they ripped my pants," Maisie gushed on about the whole experience, as we made our way inside for dinner.

"She had a wonderful time, can't you tell?" Sic asked me, as we walked together behind her. "She also wants... well, we can discuss it after dinner." He stopped to hand things off to a server before continuing to the table. "Maisie, you might want to wash your hands again," He called out, and she laughed and veered off to a small bathroom behind the stairs.

Sic followed her to wash as well, then returned to sit by me at the table. Kai and Zugo were across from us and Maisie bounced in her seat at the end. Talking rapidly, her hands gestured wildly, as she told us about feeding the baby Gryphons and their antics, "They were absolutely adorable. I can't wait to go again." The servers placed dinner down and we ate while Maisie picked at her food and rambled on.

While eating, I watched Maisie talk for several moments, distracted by her animated story. Sic's hand slid under the table and onto my thigh. I felt him slide it up toward my crotch, rubbing my cocks through my pants. It took all of my focus not to groan at the dinner table, as he worked my zipper down and slipped his hand inside.

By the time dinner was done, Maisie had told us almost every detail of their outing, minus how she had gotten holes in her pants. I suspected Sic was responsible for that detail. I was also aching for release as he had continued to stroke me, both my

cocks were hard as granite. The servers cleared the table as Zugo and Kai stood, Maisie following, still chatting up a storm as they walked off.

Once they were out of sight, Sic pulled his hand from my pants and stood. "Wanna go upstairs?" My cocks jumped at the idea of spending the night with Sic and I worked my zipper back up before I stood.

We followed the others slowly and the anticipation began to build. The guards closed the sitting room doors behind us and then I was being pressed against the wood as Sic's mouth slammed on mine. "Hey, you can't start without me," I heard Maisie's voice call from the bedroom doorway, and Sic pulled back.

"We're coming," Sic called over his shoulder and kissed me once again, softer this time.

"What do you mean, we're coming?" I had no problem with either of them but kinda wanted to know the plan.

"Let's go." Sic pulled me to the bedroom, and I noticed Kai leaning against his doorframe watching Maisie like he wanted to eat her. Zugo's door was closed, so I assumed he was going to bed.

Sic dropped my hand, while pulling Maisie to him, her back against his chest. "Does my Queen want me to strip her?" His whisper was low, and I watched Kai adjust himself on the sly, before slipping into his room. I walked closer to Maisie and Sic, glancing at Kai as I passed. He was stripping down after pulling a chair up to the doorway, to watch, no doubt.

Sic pressed kisses to Maisie's neck as he grabbed the hem of her shirt and began to lift it over her head. Her breasts sprang

free and my mouth watered as he tossed the shirt to the side. He flicked her pants open and pushed them down her hips until she was naked in front of me. He stepped back and walked around behind me. "Do you want me to fuck you while you fuck her?" His question whispered across my skin, as Maisie stepped closer to my chest.

Together they grabbed my shirt and worked it off, then Maisie flicked my button open, pushing my pants off my hips. I could hear Kai adjusting the chair for a second and I looked over to see him just as naked as she was. She walked backwards towards the bed and sat on the edge as Sic's hand stroked first one cock then the other. My head fell back on his shoulder as he continued to touch me, and Maisie spread her legs apart.

"Sic still has clothes on, Emot," Maisie teased, while sliding a finger down her slit.

"Why, sssso he doesss," I replied as I turned in his arms, dislodging his hand. I pulled his shirt off and worked his pants down, just as he had with Maisie. Once we were both naked, I pulled him closer and kissed him, our cocks rubbing together as our tongues tangled.

"This is so hot," Maisie said from the foot of the bed, making us both look over at her. She had her fingers slowly working her clit as she watched us. Kai was stroking his cocks as he watched her play with herself. Sic turned me and pushed me towards the bed, Maisie leaning back onto her elbows as we neared.

Sic watched Maisie for a moment and then softly commanded her and I, "Maisie, scoot back onto the bed, Emot eat her pussy." Neither of us argued, and I followed her as she backed up. Sic wouldn't let me crawl on the bed, so I had to pull

her towards my mouth a touch. She giggled as I pulled her, but it transformed into a moan as I bent over and licked her clit.

I began slowly, tasting her honey as she arched for more. Sic's body heat wrapped around my back as he stepped closer, his hand sliding up my back. My entire focus was on the pair of them as I feasted on Maisie and Sic began to ready my ass for his cock. Maisie lifted onto her elbows so she could watch what Sic was doing, but I kept working her clit. "One cock, Emot," Sic commanded once more, and it took all my focus to shift. Sic placed the blunt head of his enormous cock to my ass and slowly worked it past the tight ring.

The moans and groans I made, as he worked deeper, had Maisie wiggling against my mouth, so I added two fingers and began thrusting them. I barely heard the squeak of the door hinges, but didn't stop to see if Kai had shut his door or not. Sic rolled his hips, not thrusting yet; what he was waiting for I had no clue, but he felt so good in my ass. "Maisie, cum on Emot's face," He called out, and I felt her body tighten so I sped my fingers up, until she cried out in pleasure and flooded my mouth. "Good girl."

Sic grasped her ankles as I rose up a touch and pulled my fingers from her wet heat. He pulled her down below me and I felt my cock brush her pussy. Sic made sure we were lined up before pulling her down onto slowly my shaft. Her body wrapped my cock in heat and the feeling of his buried in my ass, was a breathtaking feeling. Once she had taken every inch of me, Sic pushed me down, so I covered her body. Her lips captured mine, just as Sic began to pull out of me, and then he pushed back in. His movements caused my own body to retreat and then press into hers, and we both moaned.

Sic started out slow and steady, until Maisie's moans grew steadily louder, drowning out my own groans. Eventually, he sped up, using his body to fuck Maisie with mine. He worked me

harder as Maisie's body began to tighten around me, then she screamed out and I felt her body clamp down onto mine. My own orgasm raced up my spine as Sic pounded into me. His grunt of pleasure was followed by the feeling of his cock spasming cum into my ass.

He didn't stop moving and I was locked deep into Maisie's body, unable to move. The feeling of him thrusting made the pleasure rise swiftly once more, but I tried to hold off until Maisie's body released its grip. Sic knew that I couldn't move and took advantage, pounding harder and faster. My hips slamming against her clit with his force, had her crying out again as her entire pussy clamped down around me, milking my cock for more cum. I couldn't hold back between Sic's onslaught and her body and I bit her shoulder as my cock flooded her the second time. Sic's hands tightened around my hips and then he slammed in one final time, filling me again.

Sic pulled out and collapsed onto the bed beside us as my cock remained locked deep in Maisie. I lifted onto my elbows, so I wasn't smashing her, and she smiled up at me. "We had an audience," She whispered softly, making me turn my head towards the doors. Kai was still sitting in his chair, cum coating his chest, but I was shocked to see Zugo's door cracked, as he peeked out from the gap.

Her body relaxed around me and I was finally able to slip free. I rolled onto my back on her other side much like Sic, and tried to slow my heart rate. Maisie sat up slowly, crawling to the edge of the bed and then off. Lifting onto my elbows, I watched her kiss Kai goodnight before pulling his door closed. She then slipped through the gap in Zugo's door, closing it softly.

Sic and I climbed up the bed to the pillows and he pulled me into his side. He kissed my lips and I realized I could easily go for another round, but sleep was beginning to creep in. "Later,"

He said on a yawn, and we pulled the sheets up over us and cuddled close, as sleep took over.

13

Maisie

Zugo's mouth dropped open as I slowly closed the door behind me. "Are you alright?" I asked, and he just dumbly nodded his head, his eyes locked on my naked body and I realized he had never seen a naked woman before. "Do you want me to get a robe on?" He nodded again, so I turned to leave.

"No, please don't. I'm fine and... fuck, you're gorgeous. Sorry, you don't need to dress. I just seem not to know what to say around a naked woman," He rambled adorably, while staring at my tits.

"I can get dressed if that would make you more comfortable," I offered, and he looked up at my face.

"I'm okay really, just watching you with them, was..." he trailed off, and I could clearly see he was turned on by watching. "I don't have the words, apparently." He took a step closer as if he wanted to touch me but stopped himself.

"Have you ever seen a naked woman?" I asked, and he shook his head no. "Have you ever been touched by a woman?" He nodded yes, and that threw me for a second.

Curious, I asked, "Who?"

He blushed to the roots of his hair and mumbled, "Cobra."

"What? When?" I tried to play it cool, but my basilisk hissed her displeasure at the idea of Cobra touching him.

"Right after Viper saved me from the dungeon, and all she did was give me a hand job. She flat out refused to sleep with me and she never did anything else. I still don't quite know why she did it at all," He hurried to add, as if any of that made me feel better about the situation.

"Did you ask her to?" Something felt off but I couldn't put my finger on it. Why would Cobra just do that without him asking her to? I filed that question away for later.

"No, she was helping me bathe all the grime off, and I got hard. She took care of it and that was it. It wasn't personal at all, just there and then not," He tried to explain as he walked back and sat on the end of his bed. "It was no different than if I had done it myself." He looked down at his hands and sighed.

I decided to drop the subject and walked over to him slowly. Holding out my hand for his, he placed it palm down in mine. Running my thumb over his knuckles, I turned his hand palm side up and then placed it on my chest, between my breasts. "You can touch me." I let go of his hand and stood there waiting.

My basilisk hummed her pleasure at his touch, but I could still sense her anger at Cobra for touching him. His hand slid down and over to cup the underside of my breast, as his other hand joined. Lifting them both several times, he ran his thumbs up and over my nipples. The slight contact and the coolness in his room had my nipples hardening.

His hands slid up, squeezing gently before he circled my areolas with his fingertips. He watched his every move as his

fingers ran over my skin. "May I," he cut himself off and began to drop his hands.

"Zugo, you just saw what happened in that other room, right?" He looked up at me and I could see the answer in his eyes. "You don't have to ask."

My words seemed to release some of his reserve, and he slid his hands behind my back, hugging me tight around the waist. His face was buried between my tits as he began rolling it around. "Your skin is so soft," Muffled words emerged from his mouth, just before his tongue began to lick the underside of my breast. His tongue trailed circles over one and then the other, not touching my nipples at all.

I threaded my fingers through his hair as he worked, just enjoying the innocent exploration. Finally, his tongue swiped over my aching peak and he wrapped his lips around it, sucking. Feeling his teeth scrape my skin caused me to moan softly. "Harder, Zugo." He sucked harder, but I wanted his teeth. "Bite me, please."

Zugo's teeth bit my nipple softly, but it wasn't enough, so I pulled his hair hard and his bite got harder. I cried out in pleasure as he released my nipple and flicked his tongue over it before switching to the other side. He repeated his actions with his teeth and his tongue until I ached.

"Zugo, scoot back," I said, as he released my nipple with a soft popping sound.

He slid back until he sat in the middle of the bed and I crawled up into his lap. "I hate that she touched you," He stiffened slightly at my words and was about to say something, when I pressed my finger to his lips. "So, I'm going to make you

forget she ever did." Unbuttoning his pants, I slid them down until his cocks sprang free.

I sat low on his thighs and let him resume playing with my breasts, while I slid my hands down both shafts. Beginning slowly, I stroked his cocks, pacing myself to the rhythm of him sucking on me. His moan sent tingles through my nipples as I slid my thumbs over the heads of his cocks. Precum coated my fingers as I swirled it around making his cocks twitch. I resumed stroking and he groaned. "Maisie, I think I'm going to cum."

"Then cum," I whispered, as he sucked my nipple back into his mouth. Working my hands faster he sucked harder, his groans of pleasure making me squeeze more. He hissed while biting my nipple and I felt his cocks spasm as his cum coated both my hands.

His head fell back away from my chest and he grabbed my wrists pulling my hands free. He pulled his shirt off over his head and cleaned my hands off before tossing it off to the side. "Now you're mine, and no one else will touch you," I whispered possessively, before kissing him deeply, his tongue cautiously tangled with mine.

When we finally broke apart, he was breathing heavily. "Wow, that was amazing." He kissed me again softly before quietly asking, "Would you sleep in here with me?" I smiled at his shy question and slid from his lap.

Crawling to the top of the bed, I shimmied under the covers, and he rose. I watched him pull his pants off, admiring his body, then he was sliding in next to me. He draped an arm around my stomach, his hand softly pillowed on my breast, as we both drifted off to sleep.

The next morning, I woke early and slipped out of bed, pressing a kiss to Zugo's forehead, before walking out of his room. Sic was sitting up in my bed while Emot slept. "Why are you awake?" I asked in a hushed voice, so I didn't wake Emot or Zugo. Closing Zugo's door while Sic slipped from the bed, his naked body a good morning sight, indeed.

He walked closer and handed me a robe, before heading to his own room to grab his own. When he returned, we walked to the sitting room. I noticed it was still dark out when I sat by the fire. "It was my turn to keep watch."

"What do you mean keep watch? I thought the guards did that." He sat on the couch as I leaned against it with my back. He ran his fingers through my hair as we sat, enjoying the flames.

"The guards keep the people safe, us safe, and the castle safe, but we all still guard you while you sleep. Even if it is with another one of us, Zugo has even been taking his turn since he got here," He spoke calmly, massaging my scalp rhythmically.

"We didn't have sex, if you're worried about that," I said, Knowing his jealousy might be causing him issues.

"I know," He replied simply. "You can't be quiet to save your life," He teased me, and I huffed in indignation.

"I can, too," I argued back.

"No, you can't, honey, but we all like hearing your pleasure. It means we are doing our jobs." Sic let go of my hair and I instantly missed his touch, until I felt him slide off the couch next to me. He wrapped his arm around me and pulled me closer. "Why are you up?"

"I don't know. I just woke up." The reality was, I didn't know why I was awake, I just was. "Can I ask you a question?"

"Sure, if I know the answer, I will gladly answer it," I could hear the smile in his voice.

"How did you know you loved Emot? Like, what does love feel like?" My feelings had been slowly growing for all four of these men, but I didn't know if it was love. "I'm beginning to think, I don't know what love is."

"That is a tough question." He looked into the fire for a moment then looked back at me. "I realized I was in love with Emot, when his face was the first thing I wanted to see in the morning. His smile made me smile, you were still younger at the time. As you grew up, I realized yours was the face I wanted to see in the morning. I wanted to be the one to make you smile. Emot and I don't always agree, but we work through our issues." He paused for a moment and then sighed. "As jealous as I am, seeing you with Emot is beyond erotic for me. The two people I love, loving each other, granted physically, but earlier made me realize that."

I smiled at his words as I leaned my head on his shoulder. "I think I love Emot, Kai, Zugo," I looked up and whispered the last part, "and you. Your smiles make me smile. Tour faces are the ones I want to see when I wake up. My basilisk wants to be with all of you, as well, in an almost possessive way. Just don't tell the other's yet, let them work for it a bit more."

He chuckled at my last few words and he tipped my chin up so he could look me in the eyes. "I love you, and I'm willing to wait as long as it takes for you to love me back." He pressed his lips to mine. "Let's get you back to bed, it's still too early for you to be awake." He scooped me up and carried me back to the bedroom and laid me down on the bed, before waking Emot and

kicking him out to his own room. "Sweet dreams, honey." He walked into his own room and closed the door part of the way, as I closed my eyes and tried to fall back to sleep.

Maisie

Sleep eluded me, so by the time the guys woke, I was staring at the ceiling, just waiting. Zugo yawned as he walked out of his room, but smiled as he saw me. Kai sat on the edge of the bed, waiting for something. Emot walked out of his room and peeked into Sic's before closing the door softly. "He's asleep. Kai, it's your night on watch. I'm going to make breakfast, see you downstairs." Emot pulled Zugo along with him leaving me and Kai alone.

"Did you sleep well?" Kai asked as he laid down next to me, looking at the ceiling, as well.

"There are seventy-nine wood planks in the ceiling. Does that answer your question?" He rolled over on top of me, deliberately squishing me into the mattress.

"There are actually eighty-nine, but the others are hidden around the edges." He kissed me as I pretended to groan in pain.

"You're soooo heavy. Get off." He snorted and wiggled his hips until I opened my legs.

"I'm kinda trying to, if you know what I mean," He said, as he rubbed himself on me.

"You are incorrigible. Let's go get breakfast." I tried to push his weight off me, but he somehow made himself heavier.

"We have time for a quickie." He said, as he kissed me. My laughter filled the room as he rapidly kissed my entire face, then rolled off me and sat up. "Fine, food first, fuck later. Speaking of food, do you want to go on a picnic with me?" He rose out of bed as I sat up, then he helped me stand as well. "No clothing is required if you don't wanna wear any, I won't complain."

"A picnic sounds nice, if you can get your brain off of my pussy for more than five minutes," I teased, as I fixed the robe around me, retying it tightly.

"Awe, but it's nice and warm, and my brain likes the wetness." He pinched my ass as I walked by, then we walked to the kitchens for breakfast.

Breakfast was light, and afterward, I left Emot and Kai planning for our picnic. I watched as Kai picked at food as Emot pulled things out of the fridge and laughed when Emot smacked his hand. Zugo sat next to me watching their antics. "Do you enjoy watching the three of them?" He asked suddenly, pulling my attention away from the others.

"What do you mean?" I asked, and he blushed slightly.

"Well, like last night, with Sic and Emot," He whispered, so only I would hear. I barely heard him over Emot yelling at Kai to get out.

"You mean do I like watching them have sex?" I clarified, and he nodded. "I'll be honest, it is very erotic, and I find it... I

don't know... a turn on, I guess," I answered his question as best I could.

"Would you want me to..." he trailed off and looked me directly in the eyes.

I couldn't help but laugh softly. "Not unless you want to. I'm not going to force you to sleep with them." The relief on his face was instant and almost tangible.

"I just don't think I would let them do that. I mean, I'm okay being in the room or even the bed with them, but not for that," He tried to explain, and I reached out my hand to hold his.

"You don't have to do anything you aren't comfortable with, besides, I'm not in a hurry where we are concerned, we have a ways to go, and that's okay," He smiled at my words, and then rose from the table.

"Get out, Kai!" Emot yelled, as Zugo pushed his chair in and picked up his plate.

Kai stumbled over from the force of Emot's push and plopped down into a chair. "That's so not fair," He said, and I just rolled my eyes.

"What's not fair?" Zugo took his plate to the sink and I saw Emot thank him before he walked back over.

"Emot not letting me help decide what to pack for our picnic," He huffed, as he snagged the last piece of bacon from my plate and crunched it in half. I rolled my eyes at his words as Zugo stopped by my side.

He bent low and pressed his lips to mine. "Have a wonderful picnic. I'm going to explore the village, and see if I can

help anywhere." Walking off, he left me and Kai alone with Emot in the background directing the chefs.

"I have an idea," Kai said, as he finished off my bacon.

"And what might that be?" I asked skeptically, the feeling it was going to be naughty intensified.

"Let's go shower together, get ready for our picnic so to speak." He wagged his eyebrows at me.

"I have a better idea. how about I go shower in my bathroom and you in yours, and then we can discuss other activities while we are on our date." He pouted theatrically as he sighed, but rose and cleaned up my plate.

"I guess that will work. Can you do me one favor, though?" I rose as he asked softly and arched a brow. He leaned in close, pulling me against his chest and whispered into my ear. "Drink lots of water and hold it, please." His added please was almost a desperate plea, and I shivered.

"I think I can do that, but I don't see why you'd want me to," I replied, before walking towards the exit. Kai followed me up the stairs, a grin on his face.

"You will, and I think you will enjoy it." He pinched my ass, chasing me up the stairs as I tried to run. I tried to swat at his hands, but he chased me all the way to my bathroom door and then stopped. "Remember, try not to go, and drink lots of water." He winked as he pulled my bathroom door closed, letting me shower in peace.

I tossed my robe off to the side and turned the water on, letting it warm up before I stepped in. I was curious about why Kai would ask what he did but tried not to think about it as I

showered. Once I was done, I dried off and walked naked to my closet. The day was sunny and warm, so I looked through the rack with short sundresses and pulled a light purple one out. The fabric was soft, and I decided to surprise Kai by not wearing anything underneath. I slipped on sandals before pulling my hair back in a loose bun.

When I was ready, I walked out of the closet only to have Kai standing there with a bottle of water. "Drink up." He looked over my dress and smiled. "You look beautiful."

I took the bottle from him and took a huge swig. "Are you going to be following me around all day with water?" He grinned and chuckled.

"Probably. But I promise not to be a nuisance until we leave." He laid his hand on his chest as Sic walked out of his room.

"Good morning." He yawned as he saw us standing there. "Where are you two heading?" His eye roamed over my body appreciatively.

"I'm taking Maisie on a picnic to the glade," Kai said, as Sic walked closer.

"Have a wonderful time." He brushed a kiss swiftly across my lips and then walked towards the doors. Kai pulled me close and tapped the water bottle again.

"I'll see you in a bit. I'm going to bug Emot some more." He laughed as he walked off pointing to the side table by the door. Five more water bottles were lined up there for me. I guess, he just wanted me to be hydrated.

I chugged the one in my hand and grabbed another before walking into the sitting room. Sitting on the window seat, I watched the villagers going about their day. I was people watching until it was time to leave.

15

Maisie

Kai came and got me when it was time to leave and I had polished off all six water bottles. He smiled from ear to ear when he noticed the empty bottles. "I do have to pee at this point," I hissed, as he held my hand. He carried the picnic basket in his other as we walked down the path towards the village.

We skirted the outer edge until we arrived at a path that led deep into the woods. After about twenty minutes, we arrived at a small glade with a small lake off to one side; the golden water was clear enough to see all the way to the bottom. Kai spread a blanket in the shade and placed the basket on one corner, before walking up behind me. Wrapping his arms around my waist he asked softly. "Do you want to play first or eat first? I guess, your bladder will determine that one."

I assessed my body and realized I could probably hold it a bit longer. "We can eat first." He pulled me to the blanket and began pulling a small lunch out for us. Emot hadn't packed a huge spread, and for that I was grateful.

"Would you like some basilisk mead or something else?" Kai asked, as he pulled a few bottles from the basket. His plan was becoming glaringly obvious, even though I knew exactly what he wanted.

"I guess the mead will be fine," His grin was huge as I answered, and he poured two glasses. Before he handed me one, he placed both off to the side and slid closer.

"Can I ask one serious question before we get drunk and go crazy?" His voice was hesitant, and I wondered what he might need to be serious about.

"I suppose, but you are never serious," I replied, and he rubbed the back of his neck.

"I know, and don't get used to it, but this is one thing that I feel we should take seriously," He paused for a moment and then looked into my eyes. "Will you mate with me, Margaret Day?" My lips parted and I realized I was smiling.

"I think this is the most romantic proposal I've ever heard." I realized that it was the most romantic proposal, Emot and I had just let nature take over and ended up mating, but Kai wanted my permission and it was sweet. "Yes, I will mate with you." He kissed me slowly, before pulling back and handing me a glass of mead.

"Now, we can get drunk and wild," He said, breaking the seriousness for typical Kai. He clinked our glasses together and then took a huge sip from his. I followed suit and decided, why the hell not. We were on a date, and I had to be honest, I knew what he wanted, and I wanted it, too. By the time we finished eating the small picnic, we had gone through two bottles of mead, and I couldn't hold it much longer.

"Kai, I really have to pee. Can I run off into the trees for a sec?" I asked, and he looked at me like I had lost my mind. I was slightly drunk, and the mead was making me desperate for his cocks, but the pressure was almost too much.

"Just wait two more seconds." He tossed everything back into the basket and rose. I watched him strip off his clothing swiftly, and I bit my lip enjoying the show. He knelt before me and pulled me onto my knees, lifting my dress over my head. He tossed it towards the basket as he admired my naked skin. "So, this may sound odd, but I want you to piss on me while I fuck you."

A shiver ran up my spine as his vulgar words sent excitement through my veins. Both his cocks were hard, but as I watched, he shifted them together into one massive one. He laid back on the blanket and pulled me over his lap. "Please?" He asked, as he rubbed his cock along my slit, the added stimulation made my body scream in pleasure, and the mead took over, washing my inhibitions away.

I rose up and lined him up, so his head breached my slit, before sliding down. He stretched me as I took him all in, and I felt a tiny dribble. He moaned as he felt it, too. "Gods yes, more," He begged beneath me, and I rose up again.

"I don't know if I can, Kai." He sat up on his elbows and slid his finger to my clit. He began to rub slowly while thrusting up into me. With each thrust I dribbled more, until he sat up to flip us over. The new position allowed him to work my body more and he truly began to move deep.

Each trust pushed on my bladder, and I tried to hold it but couldn't. "Just relax and let it out, sugar, please," He begged me, as he captured my lips with his. My body refused to hold it anymore and he growled as I truly began to flood his cock. "Fuck, yes," He moaned as he thrust faster. The slow release of pressure and his movements sent my body over the edge and I felt my body spasm around his, flooding him even more.

111

His cock pulsed but I didn't feel him cum as he continued to pound into me. By the time my orgasm faded, my bladder was empty, and he slowed his pace. "Gods, that felt so good," He said as he slid out of me, rubbing the head of his cock on my clit for a bit. Rolling off to the side he tucked me against his chest.

"Kai, you didn't cum," I whispered to him, as he held me tight.

"I'm not in a rush, and I have to pee now, too." He sat up as if he was going to rise and walk off. I reached out and grabbed his shoulder to stop him. "I was just going to go over there." He pointed off towards the trees.

"I... is there..." I didn't know what I was asking so I didn't know how to ask, but I was curious about this new world he had opened up for me.

"I didn't think you would want to go much further than that. I figured that might be asking for too much," He said as he rose onto his knees and turned to face me. "What do you want? I'll do whatever you wish." Sitting up, I looked at his cock and noticed he wasn't as hard as before.

"I don't know what I want Kai, this is all new to me, but I wanna try more, I guess." Kai smiled while helping me onto my knees before turning me around and pulling against him.

"Do you want me to do it on or in?" His words whispered into my neck, as his lips trailed kisses down towards my shoulder.

"You can do it in?" I asked, and he chuckled darkly.

"Yes, you can do it in." His cock rubbed at my folds as he pulled me closer still. "But I won't unless that is what you want."

"Does it cause issues with the whole sperm saving thing females do?" My voice was getting weaker, as he began to slide his hands towards my clit. His fingers swirled as he continued to nip and kiss my shoulder.

"No, cause the cum is stored deep up, it comes out if I pull out." My basilisk hissed her wishes and I slowly bent forward. "What do you want, sugar? You have to say the words," He asked, as his fingers slipped into my core.

"I wanna do it in at least once, and my basilisk is hissing for that as well, but I don't know why." I looked over my shoulder at his face and he looked like he was stunned by my choice.

Shaking himself out of his momentary stupor, I felt the head of his cock breach me and he slid about halfway in. I put my hands on the ground and he held my hips steady. "It's because basilisks mark their territory this way," He said, and then I began to feel the heat deep in my core. The feeling was more amazing than I had expected it to be, then Kai began to thrust, and I lost it. My body raced towards another orgasm as he slowly filled me in more ways than one. I could hear my basilisks purr of pleasure, and then I screamed out as my body spasmed around his.

He pulled out, and I felt the release of fluid and moaned more. "You are so fucking hot like that." His cock slid back into my pussy, harder this time, stretching me fully once more. I felt my scales pressing on my chest and knew his would be the same. Bending over, he pressed me down until he was lying on my back. "If you want to, you can shift your lower half. But only if you want to," He slowed his thrusts as he spoke, keeping his weight off me with his elbows.

He kept moving slowly, letting me decide if I wanted to mate now or later, but my basilisk took over and I felt the scales erupt over my legs. His own legs felt scaly as well and then I let

the shift take over my lower half. He held my hips tighter as his tail wrapped around mine, and he bit my shoulder softly. I could feel his hemipenes as they stroked my every nerve. They were smooth and flared at the ends, but no less pleasurable than Emot's. He didn't rush, eventually rolling me, so we were face to face.

His body rolled with mine to slide our tails together bringing my body closer to one more orgasm. He captured my lips in a deep kiss, just as my body greedily clamped onto his locking him in place. I moaned into his mouth as his body swelled and flooded mine with cum. We lay tangled up like that, neither of us wanting to move. "I love you, Kai," I whispered, as we lay there, and I felt his breath whoosh out of his chest.

"I love you, too, sugar," He said, as I placed my head on his chest, our tails still wrapped around each other. Pulling me closer to his chest, he held me as I began to doze off.

When I woke up, the sun was low in the sky and Kai's tail was still twisted around mine, but no longer connected. "I think we need to get back, sugar," Kai whispered into my hair. I shifted my legs back, feeling his shift along with mine. "But first," He trailed off, while picking me up and carrying me towards the water. He stepped into the water and walked deeper until he was chest deep.

"I figure, this way we can get clean." He held me up since my feet didn't touch the bottom unless I stood on tiptoes. "You can wrap your legs around my waist if you need to," He commented, as the warm water lapped around us.

"Yes, but if I do that you might try to take advantage of me," I teased, and he smirked.

"You're damn right I will." He slid his hands down to my ass and lifted me up until my face was level with his. "What's wrong with that?" He asked softly, before he pressed his lips to mine. "I do have one more thing to show you before we leave." I wrapped my legs around his waist as he began to walk out of the water.

I fully expected him to lift me just enough to slide both his cocks in, but he didn't, and I found myself somewhat disappointed. He set me down and pulled a towel out of the basket to wrap around me. Once I was dry, he dried himself off and packed everything up but didn't dress or hand me my clothing. "Follow me."

He led me towards the woods and up to what looked like the odd mimic plant he had told me about. Pulling me in front of him, the plant nearest my chest began moving to replicate my tits. He held me there until they stopped moving and then laughed. "Now your tits are mine forever." Digging around the base of the plant he removed the roots with a good amount of dirt and then carried it back toward the basket placing it carefully inside.

He rinsed his hands off in the water and picked up my dress and his clothing. "That's it, all you wanted was a copy of my tits?" I asked, as he handed me my dress.

Bending slightly, he licked the tip of my nipple and trailed his tongue up to my neck. "I mean, I can always keep you here longer if you want more, but I think Emot might be mad if we miss dinner, and it is getting late."

"You are such a tease." Laughing, I pushed him away and dropped my dress over my head. I watched as he pulled his pant and shirt on but left his zipper open.

"You sure you don't want one more for the road, I can make it quick." His cocks rose as he spoke, and I reached out to stroke him.

"Maybe later." I rubbed my thumb over the heads before I pulled my hand free and walked back towards the picnic blanket.

"Now, who's the tease?" I heard him say, and when I looked back over my shoulder, he was trying to get himself tucked back into his pants. He swore, and I couldn't help but laugh.

"No more than you are," I said, as he walked towards me.

"Gods, you're hot when you tease." He bent and picked up the basket and blanket so we could start our walk back. "Thank you."

"For what?" I asked, as we followed the trail back to the castle.

"For indulging me today, I can't wait to do it again." His boyish smile said more than his words could, and my own smile crossed my face. "Next time, we will do it in my bed so you can be comfortable." The castle came into view as the sun began to dip below the horizon and I saw Zugo walking back from the village.

He noticed us walking up the path and stopped to wait for us. "How was the date?" He asked when we reached him.

"We had a wonderful time," I said, and Kai snorted.

"Wonderful, I think I would say revealing, enticing, definitely mind blowing, heartfelt, soggy, but all in all, amazing." I blushed at his reference to the wet activities, but Zugo just smiled.

"I'm glad you had a great time. I'll have to think of something that can match it, for another day." We walked through the castle doors and Kai handed the blanket off to a servant before walking towards the inner courtyard and the guarders shed.

"I'm going to go replant my perfect pair of plants, I'll see you at dinner." Zugo and I watched him humming to himself as he walked off.

Emot walked up the steps from the kitchen, carrying a large tray, just as Zugo and I entered the great hall. "You're back, wonderful. I made one of your favoritesss for dinner tonight."

Sic followed with a second smaller tray and smiled. "Did you have a good time?" He tilted his head to one side and then his face blanked, but not in anger, just nothing.

Emot placed both trays on the table before noticing Sic's face. He walked over to Sic and was about to say something when he sniffed slightly. His head swung my way and he gaped for a moment, before laughing out loud. This burst of laughter snapped Sic out of his stupor and he chuckled too. Kai walked in, just as Sic and Emot's laughter died down and clapped his hands. "What's for dinner?"

We all sat down and Sic mumbled under his breath, "Not sausage, that's for sure."

"Damn, I like sausage," Kai said, not rising to the bait. Emot pulled the covers off the trays and I grinned. "Tacos, even better."

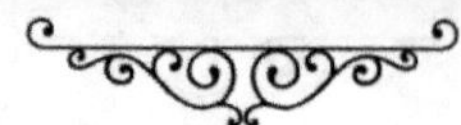

Sierin

“Yes, Emot made tacos. Now, try not to be vulgar and eat.” I knew exactly where this night was going just by the cheeky grin on his face. Maisie squealed in glee and started piling tacos on her plate and that's when Kai lost it.

“Slow down, sugar, leave some tacos for the rest of us.” Emot of all people snorted at Kai's comment and then Zugo looked up.

“I don't get it,” Zugo said, and Maisie giggled.

“He is referring to a pink taco, or a twat.” Zugo still looked confused so Kai picked up the reins Maisie had thrown down and began.

“You know cooter, bearded clam, box, cunt, vajayjay, love box, pussy, fuckhole, cunnie, meat curtains, vag, coochie, stench trench, sideways sloppy joe, fish purse, ax wound, hootenanny, poo nanny, peach, bearded oyster, puss box, sugar walls, whispering eye, juice wallet, sugar cookie, love hole, snizz, bat cave, snatch, whisker biscuit, velvet lounge, lady ham, flower, beaver, poontang pie, pun tang, tucked in beef, fanny, sea chicken taco, twat, beaver, squish mitten, pleasure ditch, crotch waffle, rocket dock, meat stocking.” Kai paused to take a deep breath and just as he was about to go on Maisie stopped him.

"I think he got it, Kai. Way to go, shocking the room."
Maisie took a bite of her taco as Kai pretended to lick his.

Zugo just looked shocked as he sat there, and I had to
explain. "They are slang words for the female body, specifically
the lower half." Clarification given, his face cleared, and he dug
into the food on his plate.

I watched Maisie enjoy her food as Emot tried to talk
about how her day had been, but Zugo interrupted once more, "Is
there slang for a guy?"

Emot groaned and Kai grinned evilly. "Don't you dare,
Kai," Was all I said, but it was too late, the flood gates had been
opened.

Taking a deep breath, Kai began. "Womb broom, womb
raider, weapon of ass destruction, trouser snake, tan banana, sex
pistol, Russell the one-eyed muscle, one-eyed monster, one-eyed
trouser trout, Rumpleforeskin, purple helmeted warrior of love,
Puff the one-eyed dragon, Prince Everhard of the Netherlands,
pleasure pump, Moby Dick, Lord Hardwick, Long dong silver, lap
rocket, Herman von Longschlongenstein, heat seeking moisture
missile, disco stick, cocktapus, clam hammer, cave hunter, mutton
dagger, yogurt slinger, meat scepter, spam javelin." He paused for
a second to breath and then began again, "Tuna torpedo, vagina
miner, Jurassic pork, the bone ranger, woody womb pecker,
nightstick, joystick, gospel-pipe, soupbone, family organ, organ
grinder, tonsil tickler, one-eyed rattlesnake, skin flute,
bushwacker, lance of love, meat skewer, crown jewels, beaver
basher, dipstick, venomous throbbing python of love,
Ramburgalar, schlong."

For a second, He looked at Maisie who was desperately
trying not to laugh. "And my personal favorite: Blood Engorged
Mayonnaise Cannon."

Maisie lost it at that moment and ended up choking on a bite of taco. "You see what you've done." I rose and began readying to do the Heimlich, but she coughed up whatever was causing the issue before I got to her. She took a long sip of her drink as soon as the coughing passed.

"Okay, no more slang at the dinner table," I said, as I returned to my seat.

"I can't believe you jussst made that rule," Emot said, as he crunched another taco.

"I wouldn't have had to if Kai could have some decency," I replied, glaring at Kai.

Maisie finished her tacos and slid her chair back. "Thank you for dinner." She kissed Emot and then me. "Have fun punishing Kai, I'm going to find Cobra. I need to ask her something." Zugo looked up with a worried face but Maisie was already gone.

"Why isss ssshe going to Cobra'sss?" Emot asked, looking at Zugo, who was somehow blushing and pale, all at once.

"I might have let it slip last night that she gave me a hand job," Zugo admitted softly, and Kai chupsed in sympathetic dismay.

"That's rough man, how'd she take it?" I asked, curious to see what Maisie's reaction to another woman touching us would be.

"She wasn't happy about it, but she seemed to push it aside and then proceeded to give me another one," He blushed at his admission, and looked around the table with wide eyes while clamping his lips shut.

Kai slapped him on the back as he rose. "Nice, man. Emot, I'll help clean up, but I have an idea for later tonight that I wanna discuss with you." Emot rose and then cleaned up the table before retreating down into the kitchens, leaving Zugo and I alone.

"I'm sorry Sic, I shouldn't have said anything," Zugo rushed out an apology, and I couldn't help but smile.

"It's fine really, you know, she's slept with those two yahoos, and you saw what happened last night, so you didn't do anything wrong," I assured him.

"I know, it is just that, I feel so inexperienced next to you three," He admitted softly, while pushing his chair back. "I guess I'm just not as sure as you three are."

I stood along with him, and we walked towards my office. "Look, if you want to learn the basic information, I have some books you can read. If you have questions, ask, Emot and I will gladly answer, and Kai will, too, after he goes on his childish rants." Opening the door to my office, I hit the light switch and instantly noticed the couch was a mess. Sighing, I walked to the bookshelf and pulled several books out, handing them to Zugo. "You can read, right?"

"Yes, I learned how before I was imprisoned," He answered, as I pulled more off the shelf and added them to the pile.

"Most of these are anatomy, basilisk and human. A few are actual sex books, like the Kama Sutra, and this one is my favorite, but don't tell the others or I will never live it down." I placed a well-worn copy of Silver Sails on top.

Zugo looked at the small stack and smiled, as I leaned against my desk. The sound of wood creaking was the only

warning I had, before the desk collapsed under me, sending me to the wood covered floor. Zugo's eyes went wide as I realized what had most likely happened, and yelled at the top of my lungs, "KAI!" Zugo placed the books on the floor and helped me up, just as Emot and Kai came running into the room.

Kai bust out laughing as Emot blanched and looked at him. "Oops," Kai said, as he wiped his eyes.

"Oops, that's all you have to say? How in the fuck did you break my desk?" I glared at him and he had the grace to look chagrined.

"Maisie and I might have, um... used it for activities," He rubbed the back of his neck as he talked, and then looked down at the stack of book. "Oh, hey, I love this book." He handed it to Zugo and said, "You should read it. it's got some great ideas."

Zugo took the book and picked the rest up, slowly walking out of the room. No doubt trying to get out of the line of fire. Emot began to pull Kai towards the door to get him away from my anger. All I could say before they walked out was, "You owe me a new desk."

Marching down to Cobra and Vipers cabin, I was about to pound on the door when it swung inward. "Come on in, Maisie," Cobra spoke, my hand hovering in midair. Walking in, I noticed it was cozy and clean, but more houses rested on the table, including two that looked like miniature castles.

Distracted for a second, I asked, "What is all this for?"

"I suspect we will be seeing more refugees in the coming weeks, so I am preparing," Cobra said, while looking at me. "I don't think that is why you are here, though."

"No. You're right. I'm here because you gave Zugo a hand job." I crossed my arms over my chest and tapped my foot.

"Yes, I did. I thought you would appreciate my gift to you," She said, and it took everything in me not to slap her.

"What gift? All I know is that you touched who is essentially my husband. In a sexual way, no less." Why did I sound so possessive? I tried to calm myself a bit by counting to ten in my head.

"Yes, a man who has been locked up for most of his life. Do you really think that is conducive to a good sex life? By now,

you have figured out that Viper and I have some magical abilities, I used said abilities to make it so he wouldn't be a two pump chump on what will essentially be your wedding night," She spoke calmly, explaining why she had done it and then walked towards her kettle. "Would you like some tea? I have a suspicion you will need it for tonight."

"Why will I need it for tonight?" She pulled two cups down from the shelf and began making me two cups of tea.

"Why would I ruin the surprise? Let's just say Kai and Emot have plans and they are wild." She handed me a cup and I took a sip, instantly knowing it was Leatherleaf. "In fact, you might want to drink a few cups." I sat at the table while she made her own tea.

"So, if you did that for me, you didn't really care about Zugo?" I tentatively asked, prompting Cobra to laugh.

"I'm a whore, a prostitute, I've only met one man who I like and that's Salzo, but he likes Viper." She sighed wistfully. "I like Zugo, he is a nice boy, but I don't want him in that way, if that is what you are asking. It took him like three strokes, and he came. I'm good but not that good." She laughed at herself and sat next to me. "I did truly have you in mind when I added that magic. You've had such a disappointing sex life up until now, I thought you deserved an all-around amazing one now."

Sipping my tea, she stuck her finger under the bottom and tipped the cup more making me chug it. Her eyes clouded over for a moment, then cleared. "Forget the tea, you're going to need something stronger." She rose and grabbed a clear glass and pulled several jars off the shelf. I watched in awe as she pulled things out and added it to the glass. When she was done adding herbs, she pulled a green bottle off the table and poured a full

glass. The liquid turned black and bubbled for a moment before settling.

"It's bitter and takes about twenty minutes to work but I think you're gonna need it. Chug it down fast." She handed me the glass and I looked at the black ooze looking liquid. "Just drink it, I use it all the time with my customers."

I sniffed the contents before taking a sip, it made me gag as it slid down my throat. "That's why I said chug it." Screwing up my courage, I chugged the glass as fast as possible. The flavor was bitter and reminded me of licorice but not the good kind, the nasty black stuff. "There you go, now get your ass up to bed and have fun."

Cobra practically pushed me out of her cabin, and I walked the path up to the castle. I began to feel a slight tingle just as I entered the main doors. By the time I made it to the bedroom, I could feel myself dripping on my inner thigh. The desire racing through me was almost too much, and as I looked up, I saw Kai and Emot sitting naked in my bed, side by side.

"Welcome home, darling," Emot spoke up from the bed. Sic's door was open but he wasn't in there, while Zugo stood off to one side, grinning like a loon. He was just as naked as they were.

My mouth watered at the sight and my body was on fire. Crawling up the bed, Emot's fingers went to the hem of my dress, as Kai plundered my mouth. He pulled back and looked at me oddly. "She didn't." Emot pulled my dress over my head and the evidence of my need was coating my thighs.

"Ssshe did," Emot said to Kai, while sliding a finger along my slit. I cried out as he swirled my clit before sliding two finger

in. Pulling them out, he held them out to Kai who licked them clean.

"Holy fuck, that's hot." I moaned as I watched Kai suck Emot's fingers. Emot's hand returned to my pussy and he began spreading my wetness around everywhere including my ass. I was so wet that when his hand rubbed me, he slipped in twice.

"Cobra gave you a Rushed Nightfall, didn't she?" Kai asked, and Emot's eyes snapped to mine. I nodded as I watched them scoot closer together, the bedroom door closed, and I looked over my shoulders to see Sic locking them. His robe was open, and I could see his cocks. He peeled off his robe and tossed it towards the wall as Emot turned me around to face the room.

When I looked back over my shoulder, Kai and Emot were seated cocks to cocks their legs tangled together. They pulled me back easily holding me above their laps. "This is going to be one hell of a ride, sugar. Are you ready?"

"Hurry up before I die," I said, and Kai laughed as they lowered me. One of Kai's cocks and one of Emot's parted my dripping pussy, stretching me gloriously. I wanted them to move but they only lifted me up slightly and I felt two cock press against my ass. My wetness coated them and them allowing them to slip in easily. My moan was instant as they filled both my pussy and my ass.

Sic watched from the end of the bed as they began to lift me up before dropping me down. Each stroke made me moan and my back arched slightly as they pulled my legs wide open. Sic could see them fucking me as he crawled up onto the bed. Zugo walked towards the side to get a better look.

Kai's voice slid over my skin as they lowered me again. "Sic is going to eat your pussy while we fuck you," The moment

the words were said, I felt Sic's tongue lick my clit. Emot and Kai groaned as I felt myself tighten around them. Sic swirled his tongue over me and I could feel him lick the guys as well, making me even wetter, if that was possible. My orgasm began to build as he sucked my clit between his teeth and then I felt his forked tongue slip into the gap between Emot's and Kai's cocks. I screamed loud as I shattered around them.

"Fuck, ssshe'sss gonna wake the whole village. Zugo, give her sssomething to sssuck on." Emot motioned for him to climb onto the bed. "Can you ssshift to one cock?" He asked, and I watched Zugo's twin cocks combine into one. He stepped over Sic nervously until Emot pulled him closer.

"Be a good girl and sssuck hisss cock," He hissed into my ear, as they continued to move me. I reached out and grasped the base of Zugo's cock as he balanced himself on Emot's and Kai's shoulders, standing over Sic. Pulling him closer, I licked the head of his cock and he groaned, then I opened wide and sucked him in. My basilisk decided to shift my jaw just enough so I could take every inch of his cock, deep into my throat.

The feel of all four men touching me, set my nerves on fire. Each touch bringing with it more ecstasy than I knew could exist. A second orgasm raced through me and I flooded Sic's face as I let Zugo thrust into my mouth. I couldn't scream with him in my mouth, but my moan set his own moan off, as it sent vibrations through his cock.

I glanced at Sic as best I could around Zugo's cock and noticed him stroking his own cocks. Letting Zugo slip out for a moment, I hissed at Kai and Emot, "Sssomeone help him." I pulled Zugo back into my mouth and let my own forked tongue swirl around him as he began to thrust. Kai and Emot adjusted their grips, so they each had a hand free, and I heard Sic growl as

his forked tongue continued to play with my clit before sliding in and then back again.

Sic's moans sent vibrations up through my clit and I felt my body tighten once more. Zugo grunted as his hand tightened in my hair, and I felt his cock spasm on my tongue. Hot cum slid down the back of my throat setting my own orgasm off, once more. My body clamped down on Kai and Emot, milking them both. Kai hissed his pleasure as they both spasmed, filling my ass and pussy at the same time. I sucked harder on Zugo making him cum a second time and loving every second of it.

Zugo slumped to the bed beside Emot's back as Sic rolled over, cum coating his chest and the covers. Kai and Emot were locked tight in my body for the moment but they both slumped against me, sandwiching me in a tight hug. Once my body relaxed, I felt them lift me and place me up on the pillows. The second my head touched down; I was dead to the world.

18

Maisie

When I woke the next morning all four of the guys were still in the bed with me. Emot and Kai still had their legs tangled together, Zugo was hanging off the side of the bed, and Sic was sprawled across the bottom. Emot was wide awake when I went to sit up, but Kai's arm was a solid weight on my chest. Emot picked up Kai's arm so I could move again and helped me up. "Why are you awake?" I whispered, as I climbed over him.

He pulled me down for a tender kiss, before whispering back, "My night on watch." I slid over Zugo trying not to wake him, but he rolled as I was almost over him, and we both tumbled to the floor. "Owe." Emot looked over the side of the bed at Zugo and me. Zugo's face was between my legs his face buried in my crotch.

I watched as Kai's and Sic's heads popped up next to Emot's and Kai laughed. "Well, that's one way to wake up in the morning."

Zugo pushed himself up and began apologizing. "It's fine, I'm not hurt," I assured him, and he blushed when he realized where his face was.

"You could always give her a morning wake up," Kai said before he grunted, as Sic hit his shoulder.

"Leave him alone," Sic chided, and I sat up climbing to my feet.

"Good morning to all of you. I'm going to shower. And no, Kai," I said, before he could ask to join me.

"Ssshe hasss you pegged," Emot spoke, as I walked to my bathroom. I took a long shower, enjoying the feel of the warm water. My body was sore but in the most glorious way, and I stood for a moment just remembering last night.

A knock on my door had me turning the water off. "Maisie, may I come in?" Zugo's voice passed through the wood as I grabbed a towel.

"Sure," I called back, and he opened the door slowly.

"I wanted to see if you would like to go for a walk later this morning. Maybe meet the Sprites. My mom used to spend a lot of time with them, and they are really nice." He fiddled with the door handle as he asked, "But only if you want to."

Wrapping the towel around me I walked towards the door. "I would love to, but let's get breakfast first." He nodded as I walked by, heading for my closet. I could feel him watching me as I rummaged through my drawers for underwear. "Did you need something else?" My question was soft, so he didn't feel like he was doing anything wrong.

"No, I just can't get over last night and how beautiful you looked. How beautiful you look now," His words made me blush, and I dropped the towel deliberately.

"You don't have to hover by the door." He smiled but didn't move.

"I know, but if I get closer, I will want to touch you, and you need to eat, so I don't want to distract you," His explanation was more of a ramble. I realized he was still nervous about the sexual aspect of our relationship. I pulled my clothes on faster after that and then grabbed his hand.

"Let's go eat. Then we can go for a walk." We walked down the stairs together to get food.

Zugo and I left through the main gates just after breakfast. The walk wasn't long, and we took a similar path that Kai and I had taken the other day. Once in the coolness under the trees, Zugo grabbed my hand, lacing our fingers together. "You're okay with me holding your hand, right?" He asked nervously, and I chuckled.

"Zugo, I sucked your dick last night, you can do more than hold my hand," I replied, as he blushed. Changing the subject, so he wasn't uncomfortable, I asked, "So, the Sprites where do they live?" He smiled as we walked into a small stand of trees forming a tight circle.

"They live here, up in the treetops." Several small lights fluttered down, and a beautiful man with green hair, bowed deeply in my face.

"Your Majesty, welcome to Honeyhall, my name is Stone Copperwhisk. I am Her Majesties advisor, and she would like for me to welcome you to our small Kingdom. If you would like, I can shrink you and you may join us in the trees." I looked over at Zugo and he shook his head no.

"Thank you for the offer, but I would like to remain here," I spoke softly, so I didn't hurt the tiny man's ears.

133

"Of course, Her majesty will be down momentarily," He replied before fluttering off.

"Why can't we shrink?" I whispered to Zugo, but he was looking up.

"Because the spell lasts for several weeks and we don't have weeks to be tiny," He replied, as several more Sprites floated down. He looked over at me and smiled. "I promise to bring you back sometime, when we can safely remain here for some time and then you can visit them for a while." Zugo and I sat down in the center of the trees to wait.

I smiled at that, thinking about what the future might hold, if only we could truly have peace in Lasina. My father was making that difficult, and I suspected he was just getting started. Several Sprites fluttered over and Zugo held out his hand for them to sit down. "Zugo, my, how you have grown," The tiny grandmotherly voice called out.

"It has been a very long time, Freesia, how are you and your children?" He asked back, as another Sprite landed on my head, playing with my hair.

Freesia replied to Zugo's question, while several other pixies began to fiddle in my hair. I felt one rolling around, as two more picked up long strands and tugged. "What are you doing up there?" Since I couldn't see the top of my head, I had no clue.

Freesia's laugh had me turning to look at her. "They are not used to so much hair, Your Majesty. They are playing in it, take it as a compliment. they wouldn't play in it, if it wasn't soft and silky." She fluttered up to my head and shooed the others away. "There now, you might need a good brushing when you get home," She said, as she sat back down on Zugo's palm.

A bright light lit the space and Freesia stood, bowing as the light got closer to us. I held out my hand and two tiny feet tickled my palm. "Your Majesty, it is an honor to meet you." The light faded and a small woman with navy blue hair held out her hand. I stuck my pinky out and she shook my finger. "My name is Dandelia Starweather, and this is my Kingdom."

"It is nice to meet you, Your Majesty. My name is Margaret Day, but you may call me Maisie." She smiled brightly and then flopped down onto my hand, sitting cross-legged.

"Thank you for including our Kingdom within the walls. your father hates Sprites, and we were forced to flee his lands. Thankfully, your kings allowed us full use of these woods," She spoke up so I would hear her, but I could still hear the sadness in her voice.

"Are you the only Sprite Kingdom in Lasina?" I asked, while she wiped an eye.

"Oh no, we are but one of many. I believe there are six more in these woods alone. See, Sprites are much like bees, we tend to the flowers and plants, but each hive has a Queen. My mother is Freesia, I am her eldest daughter. When she retired new male Sprites arrived and I began the breeding of more sprites." She smiled and waved an arm around at the houses.

"Oh, so you are the only one who can produce children then?" I asked, wondering if it was like a true beehive.

"Every female here is either my sister or my daughter. The males come and they can mate, but only I can actually have children. My older daughters have gone out and started hives of their own. Once I retire, my oldest will take over here," She explained and then tapped her lip. "Unlike bees, we do grow a lot slower, I can only have two children a year. But I will admit,

trying for those two is always fun." She giggled softly and I saw Zugo blush slightly.

Freesia flew over to my palm and plopped down next to Dandelia. "You shouldn't speak that way, Dandelia," She spoke softly, but I could still hear.

"Mother, she has four Kings, I think she understands." She looked my way and I couldn't help the grin that crossed my face. "See, she gets it."

"MAISIE!" I heard Sic's voice yell through the trees. Freesia and Dandelia fluttered off my hand and I rose.

"We are over here, Sic!" I yelled back in the direction of the path. His face came into view and I instantly noticed something was wrong. "What happened?"

"Vago has attacked more of the Eastern Kingdom. More people are arriving and several need medical help. He is escalating and Emot's parents had to flee their lands," Sic explained quickly.

I turned to look at Dandelia. "I am sorry, but I must go."

"I understand, and please let us know if we can help," She replied, as Zugo and I began making our way to Sic. When we reached the path, Sic began running back towards the castle and we followed.

Maisie

Streams of people began to arrive through the side gates, many injured. Sic and Cobra had their hands full trying to help those most in need, while castle medics helped those with less injuries. Emot found me just as his parents' carriage rolled through the gates. "Cobra hasss housssesss and more wallsss for the new arrivalsss, but with all the injured, it might take a few daysss to get everyone sssettled. My parentsss can ssstay in the cassstle with usss until they have a new place, and the townsssspeople are helping othersss until homesss become available."

"I know basic first aid. If you, Kai, and Zugo help her with the homes, I can help with Sic for a bit. That way at least some of these people will have a place," I said, as I began walking towards Sic and Cobra.

"Good idea, Maisie. You take my place here and listen to Sic, let's go Emot," Cobra spoke from beside me, before I even reached her. Once I was standing next to Sic, he had me working up a storm. He healed life threatening wounds, and I patched up the easier ones.

Emot's parents joined in, and by the time the sun started to set, the last of the arrivals were patched up and sent to a new home. "Cobra did amazing," Sic said, as he looked out over the

new homes. The walls had been expanded out even more, creating a large city around us.

"Really, Sic. Why don't you go marry her!" I snapped, before turning back towards the path up to the castle.

He rushed after me and pulled me to a stop. "What's wrong? You know that isn't what I meant."

Sighing, I looked up into his eyes. "I'm sorry, I shouldn't have snapped. I'm just tired, and hangry. You are correct, she did do a wonderful job."

"Let's get you something to eat, and then I'll run you a bath. Sound good?" He asked, as we began walking back to the castle again.

Emot's parents had gone back earlier, when Cobra had finished with the houses, and returned to helping the injured. They both stood on the steps of the castle waiting for us. Escu pulled me into a tight motherly hug as she thanked me over and over, soothing some of my anger. "I bet you are starving. dinner is ready, so we can all sit down to eat." She pulled me inside and the smells that filled the air had my stomach growling.

The servers placed the trays on the table as we arrived, and I sat down in my seat as Emot dished out the food. I didn't taste a single thing as I ate swiftly, and if anyone talked, I didn't hear, until after I had cleaned my plate. "Thank you for letting us stay here, Maisie," Evat spoke up, making me jump in my seat.

"You are welcome," I spoke, as I debated on licking my plate. Emot must have sensed my thoughts as he offered me more food to keep me from doing just that.

"Cobra mentioned that she has a larger home ready for the two of you once we settle on a location," Sic spoke, and I dug in to the second helping.

By the time dinner was over, I was stuffed and trying not to yawn at the table. Emot rose and offered to show his parents to a guest room for the night, while Sic walked towards me. "Let's get you upstairs." He picked me up and carried me towards the room as Kai and Zugo followed.

"It's my night on watch, right?" Kai asked, as the guards opened the door to the sitting room.

Zugo opened the bedroom doors as Sic looked back for a moment. "Yes." He walked towards my bathroom before setting me down and opening the doors. Zugo disappeared into his bedroom, as Kai took over for Sic, picking me up. He sat on my dressing stool holding me as Sic started the water. "Okay, put her down and go do something else." Kai let me stand just before Sic pushed him out the door and locked it.

Sic turned back to me before walking closer and helping me strip down. Once I was naked, he helped me into the tub. The warm water began to work the knots out of my back. "Is the temperature okay?" He asked, as he knelt by the side of the tub.

"Yes, it's perfect." My eyes closed as I leaned back on the side of the tub. Cracking one eye just enough to see Sic, I commented offhandedly, "You know, you can get in here with me." He smiled but I watched him rise and begin to strip down.

He turned to toss his clothes on the seat, and I noticed the scar on his hip, once again. I slid forward in the water and trailed a finger across the pale white lines, causing him to stiffen. "What happened here?" I asked, as he turned and stepped into the tub behind me.

"It's old and nothing to worry about," He brushed it off, trying to pull me back against his chest.

I turned, so I was facing him, my legs over his. "I want to know what happened. I have a right to know, don't I? You keep telling me we are married. So, as your wife, I want to know." I slid closer to him, hugging his neck loosely.

He lifted me slightly and placed me in his lap before sighing. "Back when we first started sleeping together, my mother caught Emot and I in bed together. She has always had a temper, and she lost it," He trailed off, as if reliving that day in his mind.

"What happened when she lost her temper?" I asked quietly, trying not to disturb his thoughts.

"She has some ability with lightning spells, and she aimed one at Emot. I curled around him and took the brunt of it. All the while she was yelling about the treaty, and the family. When she realized she had hit me instead of Emot, she froze in shock." He pulled me closer to his chest, rubbing my back as he spoke. "She left after that and told me to end the relationship. We had already begun this place, so I just moved out here and Emot came with me."

I looked up into his eyes, and while there was a sadness there, I didn't see regret. The feeling of his cocks between our bodies, as he pulled me closer still, had my core aching with need. Trying to ignore the ravenous beast between my legs, I asked, "Who helped you heal?"

"Emot made sure it was clean, and I used my healing magic to close it as much as possible. I wasn't as practiced with it then, as I am now." He tipped my chin up and looked me in the eyes. "Enough about the past."

He pressed his lips to mine, while pulling me fully against his cocks. I couldn't help but rub my slit on his hardness as his tongue fenced with mine. Sic's hands slid around to my chest and he cupped both my breasts, rubbing his thumb over my nipples. I reached down between us and stroked both his cocks with my hands causing him to break our kiss. We both gasped for breath as I began to rise onto my knees. Just as I was about to position him so I could slide down, he stopped me.

"Not yet. I know you're not ready and I don't want you to do it just to make me feel better." He pulled my hands away from him and I pouted, making him chuckle. "I didn't say we couldn't play; I just don't want you to regret the choice."

"I wouldn't regret it, Sic. I want you just as much as the others." His hand slid up my thigh and his fingers swirled my clit. My head fell back on a groan as he began to tease me.

"Fine, you might not regret it, but I still don't think now is the right time," He spoke calmly, as he slid two fingers into my pussy. "If you want, we can move to the bed," His seductive whisper blew cool air across my nipple, just as he flicked his tongue out to tease the hard peak.

"Did you know that a basilisk's tongue is just as thick as a human cock and can be used as such?" He spoke offhandedly, while rising from the water. His cocks were at my eye level and I couldn't help but flick my tongue out and lick both heads as he stood. "Come on, let's go to bed."

"I wanted to play in the water more." I pretended to pout, and he laughed as he climbed out. He pulled the drain and then helped me stand. Once out, he wrapped me in a towel and dried me off.

"I can't breathe under water, and what I have in mind requires a bed." Sic dried off before tossing both our towels off to the side. He picked me up and carried me not to my bed but his, and placed me gently in the center. I watched him reach for something on the side of the bed only to see him pull a restraint up. He fastened it around my wrist before doing the other three limbs, leaving me spread-eagled on the mattress.

Walking to the bottom of the bed, he admired my position before crawling between my legs. He flicked his tongue out and I gasped at the size. When he was playing with my clit, I never noticed its size since he only used the tips. He trailed his tongue up first one thigh and then the other. His hand pressed my knees to open wider and he laid down between them, pressing a kiss to my slit. "Ready?" He asked but didn't wait for an answer, as he slid his full tongue into my pussy.

The size was, indeed, similar to a human cock, and he wielded it with precision. His hands trailed up my body, pinching my nipples while he thrust his tongue. My body didn't care what was bringing it pleasure and I writhed in the bindings as he worked me up. I begged for release, but he kept me just on the edge. His fingers trailed down towards my slit and then he pinched my clit, sending me over the edge.

I moaned as my body spasmed around his tongue, only to have him curl it more and move faster. The change in his movements began to rub my g-spot and I knew what he was aiming for. He pressed upward harder as he stroked, and the pleasure built along with the pressure. When he sped up again, my body shattered, clamping down onto him while simultaneously flooding his face. He hummed his appreciation, and the vibration sent me higher still.

"Sic, please. I need your cocks now," I begged, but he just kept working me, rubbing his fingers along my clit. He ignored my pleas for his cocks, but I felt his other hand slide towards my slit.

"I'll give you more, but you aren't getting my cocks tonight," His almost sinister voice had me shivering, as he readjusted and knelt between my legs. He began to stroke himself with one hand while he worked the fingers of his other hand into my core. He shifted his cocks into one to make it easier as he began to work more fingers into me. He made me cum two more times before he pulled his hand free, my body relaxed, and yet, I felt unfulfilled.

He slid closer, and I prayed he would break and slide his cock into me, but he didn't. He just used the head to tease my clit, rubbing up and down as he stroked himself more. I tried to reach down, but the bindings wouldn't let me move much. His face was a picture of pleasure as he neared his own orgasm, rubbing me faster. My own body begged for him to cum, and then I felt his head barely part my slit as hot cum filled my pussy. "Fuck." He moaned as more cum flooded me and then he pulled away.

He untied my legs first, and then my hands, before laying down beside me. "How can you have that much control?" I asked, making him laugh.

"Magic requires a lot of control and once you learn to be in control, it never goes away." He pulled me to his chest, and I placed my head over his heart.

"Does that count as consummation if you came inside me?" I asked, looking up at his face.

He used his foot to pull the covers over us and then did an odd flicking motion with his finger and the light went off. "On this, I will have to agree with Kai, just the tip doesn't count." He

chuckled and I scoffed at his words, before he began rubbing my back. "Sweet dreams, honey." I began to drift off as his heartbeat lulled me to sleep.

I listened to Sic make Maisie cum over and over again, tormented by the fact that I was on watch. Sic knew if I were allowed in there, I would pass out afterward. Rules sucked, and his need for control sucked even more, sometimes. His muffled 'Fuck' came through the door, so I rose and walked towards the sitting room. Cobra stood in the doorway for a moment, her head cocked to one side, then she noticed me.

"He still hasn't slept with her," She said, while walking further into the room. "I need to speak to you, about a sensitive matter." I sat on the couch while she made herself comfortable in the chair.

"And what might that be, giving hand jobs to Maisie's mates?" She glared at my cheap shot but then smiled.

"I gave him more stamina to be able to pleasure your mate. You, on the other hand, don't need it." She looked me up and down, assessing my body like a piece of meat, or a client.

"Hey, as long as you squared it away with Maisie, I don't care. So, what's so important that you had to wait until I was the only one awake to come here?" If it wasn't important and Maisie found out, Cobra wasn't the one who would have issues.

"Salima just hired Viper to kill your father," Her words floored me, and I stood up.

"What!" I yelled, only to remember too late that everyone was asleep. Zipping my lips, I listened for a moment but didn't hear anything, so I hissed again, "What do you mean?"

"Viper has been following Salima for the last few days; she had a suspicion that Salima was up to something. What, I don't know, so don't ask." She paused for a moment, looking into the flames in the hearth. "She contacted me tonight about a plot to kill your father. Viper was hired by one of Salima's servants. She left the servant for now, and is currently on her way to warn your father. She told me she will go back for the servant after she 'takes your father out'."

All I could do was pace the floor, as Cobra told me all of this. My father was now being targeted, but why would Salima do that? "Are you sure Salima is the one behind this plot, and not some other noble?" I stopped pacing and looked at her.

"The servant is Salima's personal manservant," She replied, and I knew Sic would be pissed when he found out. "You can't tell the others what you know. Wait until your father arrives and Viper returns with the servant. Let her tell Sic, I doubt it will surprise him much."

"When is she supposed to return here?" I asked, trying to gauge how long I would have to keep this secret.

"Tomorrow evening, the beauty of our kind is that we can travel fairly swiftly. Now, if you will excuse me, I have a busy day ahead of me tomorrow." She rose from the chair and began walking to the doorway. "You can tell Emot, if you need to tell anyone, besides, he can help you take care of that." She pointed to my crotch, then walked out of the door, closing it behind her.

I paced for several minutes, realizing that even the idea of my father being in peril didn't dampen the need that Maisie's and Sic's noises had caused. I walked into the bedroom and opened Emot's door. He was wide awake, naked, and just as hard as I was. He was lazily touching himself and I closed the door behind me. "Why are you here?" He asked, as he paused his hand.

"Lots of reasons." I didn't bother explaining as I pulled my shirt off over my head. "I need to fuck something, or I'll go crazy." He barked a laugh and nodded.

"They got to you too?" He sat up as I tossed my pants off to the side and shifted my cocks to one.

"This isn't going to be gentle," I warned, as I grabbed his ankles and pulled him to the end of the bed.

"Fine by me, fassst and hard it isss," He replied, as I began pressing in. I gave him about half a second to adjust before I slammed forward. His cocks pulsed as he stroked himself and I pounded his ass hard. "Harder. Kai," He moaned, making me slam even harder and faster.

Sweat began to drip off my forehead and onto his body thanks to my bruising pace, and then he groaned as cum shot up his abs. His body clamped around mine and I kept pounding until I filled him twice. I wiped the sweat off my head as I pulled out and sat beside him on the bed. "What? Not going to passss out now?" He teased, as he sat up next to me.

"Viper was hired to kill my dad," My whisper was barely audible, and he looked my way. "She won't do it, of course, but Cobra said Salima was involved."

"Holy ssshit." He stood up and picked up my pants, handing them over. "We need to tell Sssic."

"We can't. Viper will be back tomorrow night. Besides, let him have his time with Maisie." I pulled my pants on and zipped them up. Emot nodded as if agreeing, but I could still see the indecision in his eyes. "Cobra said to let Viper tell Sic."

"Okay, I won't sssay a word. Wanna crasssh in here for a bit? I won't tell Sssic, I ssswear." I laughed at his offer.

"You're just hoping for a round two." He had the nerve to arch his brow and look at my crotch.

"One of these daysss, I'm going to get you to take me, and you're gonna love it," He teased me, and I rolled my eyes. "Well, maybe you would sssuck me at least. Imagine what Maisssie would do if you sucked my cock for her."

"We'll see. If Maisie asks then yes, I would, but only for her, not for you." I scooped up my shirt and pulled it back on before walking to the door. "Thank you, Emot."

"You're alwaysss welcome, you know that," He said, as I opened his door and slipped back out, closing it behind me. Walking back into the sitting room, I sat on the couch and stared off into the fire.

21

Maisie

When I woke the next morning, Sic was still holding me in the position we had fallen asleep in. His steady breathing told me he was still asleep, so I snuck out from under his arm and tiptoed out of the room. Kai was sitting on the couch but everyone else was still asleep. My bladder yelled at me as I tiptoed across the room, until Kai called out, "Why are you up?"

I froze in my tracks and looked at him as he rose from the couch and walked towards me. Dancing in place for a moment, until he stopped in front of me. "Why are you awake? It's still early."

"Gotta pee." He laughed softly and scooped me up, walking into the bathroom. I fully expected him to leave once I was in there, but he sat down on a chair with me straddling his lap. He slid his hand down my chest, tweaking my nipples before continuing down to my clit.

"Have at it, sugar," He said, while rubbing slow circles around my clit.

"You're dressed Kai, are you crazy?" I said, as my bladder began to ache more, and his fingers slipped lower.

"I am very well aware of the fact I'm dressed, and I want you to. Would you feel better if I slid my cock in your pussy?" His dirty words made me shiver, as his fingers began to thrust into me. "Piss on me, sugar," He commanded, and I moaned as he began to stroke me.

My body chose that moment to release the floodgates and he sped his hand up as I began to pee. "That's it, sugar, let it all go." He worked faster and my body began to tighten. His lips captured my nipple and he bit down softly, and I cried out as I orgasmed around his fingers, gushing even more.

He slid his hand free and rocked me on his cocks, growling as the wet heat turned him on more. "I wanna fuck you so bad right now." He captured my lips as my body finally finished coating him.

He leaned back and looked down smiling at the mess I made. "If I could wake up to this every morning, I would." Picking me up higher, he unbuttoned his pants and positioned his cocks at my pussy letting me slide down both. My tiptoes barely touched the ground until he closed his legs some so I could stand. "Ride me, sugar. Good and hard."

Grasping the back of the chair I rose up and slid back down, starting slow as he sucked my nipples. His hands on my hips began to push me down faster, and I sped up until I was bouncing on his cocks, my body greedily begging for more. I began to feel more wetness and then his cocks flooded my pussy as I came hard. I had to bite my lip to keep from screaming out my pleasure and Kai rolled up into me harder.

He picked me up suddenly, and all I could do was hold on tight. He pushed his pants off his hips and kicked them to the side. "I got you, but I need you to take my shirt off." Not bothering to stop lifting me up and down, I pulled the hem of his shirt up.

Juggling me from one hand to the other we worked his arms out, until he was free of the shirt. Walking to the shower, he opened the door and stepped in. He faced me away from the water and turned it on, waiting until it was warm before stepping in.

Holding tight around his neck he worked me harder as warm water trailed over our skin. "Cum on my cocks," He growled, as he began to slam into me, hard and fast. My body responded instantly and before I knew it, I was milking his cocks again, moaning into his neck. He pumped a few more times before biting my shoulder as he growled his release.

Once my body released his, he slid out and set me on the ground, making sure I was steady before letting go. "Today is going to be a busy day, so I wanted to make sure it started out on a good note," His words were cryptic, and I was just about to ask what he meant, when Sic slammed the door open.

"Kai, your father just arrived. Saying something about an assassination attempt." Kai sighed before getting out and drying off.

"I'll see you later, sugar." He walked out of the bathroom, leaving Sic standing in the doorway staring at me. I turned the water off and stepped out to dry off. Sic noticed the pile of wet clothes and raised an eyebrow in question.

"Do you really want to know?" I asked, as I walked towards him. He followed me to my closet and stopped in the doorway as I searched for clothes.

"It's Kai, and it wouldn't be the first time he's asked for that. Emot is usually the one to oblige, but if you enjoy it, I can only imagine what the three of you could get up to," He said, as I dressed. "Kai's father's name is Jeca, just to remind you." I walked to the door and stopped next to Sic.

"Does it bother you that I enjoy it?" I asked shyly, afraid he might say yes.

"No, and I would do it, for you, if that's what you wanted. It just isn't my thing, but that doesn't mean I'll judge you for it. Emot has his own likes just like Kai and I. I'm sure once Zugo figures himself out, he will have his own as well. There is nothing to be ashamed of, you like what you like and that's okay." He tipped my chin up so I was looking into his eyes. "I love you regardless."

He was about to kiss me when I whispered, "I love you too, Sic." What I expected to be a tender kiss turned heated at my admission, and I had to grab the door frame to keep from losing my balance as my knees went to Jell-O.

"We should go help Kai and Jeca." He stepped back and let me walk out the door first. The day was going to be just as Kai had said it would be, and I sighed.

Jeca was sitting in the great room with Emot's parents and Kai when we arrived downstairs. The sun had just risen and Emot was in the kitchens still getting breakfast ready. Zugo walked up the stairs carrying a jug of what looked like juice, followed by a server with glasses. "Emot says breakfast will be up in a moment," He said as he placed the jug on the table.

I sat in my normal seat as Jeca began to speak again, "Viper told me that there was a bounty on my head, and that she had been hired via servant to kill me. I don't understand why, though, or who."

"Did Viper say anything else?" Sic asked, as Emot brought breakfast up. The servers put the plates out as Emot sat at his place.

"She said that whoever was responsible would be brought here this evening. I believe she was going to tell them I was dead and then bring them here. I just don't know how she would be able to do that," Jeca spoke, as we passed the plates around.

"Well, Dad, you are welcome to stay here. How is everyone else?" Kai asked, as Jeca took a bite of food, surprisingly in high spirits even after having someone trying to kill him. I

began to notice the similarities in their looks as I watched Kai and Jeca.

Cobra walked in while I was busy, looking at the two men, and she cleared her throat. "Your Majesties. Maisie, might I borrow you for a bit?"

Jeca gaped at Cobra. "I thought you wouldn't be here till tonight," He said, his boisterous voice filling the room.

"Jeca, this is Cobra, Viper's twin sister," I said, introducing them as I rose. "If I am not needed, I'll go help Cobra and be back later." I kissed each of the guys before I walked beside Cobra towards the door.

"That one is a keeper," Jeca said just loud enough that I heard, and Kai groaned. "The blonde isn't too bad either, eh, son." I heard a grunt from Kai as if his dad had elbowed him in the gut. I tried not to laugh at Jeca, then noticed that Cobra was blushing.

We walked in silence until we were outside, and she fanned herself. "That man," Was all she said, as we followed the path towards her cabin and the Nymph lake. "I have been thinking of suitable placement of the Eastern King's home as well as Jeca's and I thought we might ask the Nymphs." It was not lost on me that she called Jeca by his first name, but not Evat and Escu.

"I think that is a wonderful idea," I replied, but then curiosity got the better of me. "Did Jeca love Kai's mother?"

"I believe theirs was an amiable relationship, however, it lacked true passion the way the Eastern King's marriage does. Evat loves Escu dearly, and it shows in how he treats her. Jeca and Kimma were very well matched, but they lacked the love needed for true harmony." She walked towards the golden lake and tossed a small stone into the center.

Within a few minutes, bubbles appeared along with a suction cup covered tentacle. Only the king was present, and he rapidly grew to the full height, so we could speak. "Good morning, Your Majesty." He tipped his head in respect before turning to Cobra. "Cobra, good morning to you, too."

"We would like to discuss the placement of a few larger homes with you for the Southern King and the Eastern King and Queen," Cobra spoke politely. "We thought the lands around your lake would be open enough for the homes, but don't want to intrude on your space."

"As long as they aren't in the water itself, it doesn't intrude on our space. It will be an honor to have such neighbors," He spoke, and I smiled.

"Thank you so much, Your Majesty." He held his hands out and took mine before placing air kisses on both my cheeks.

"Let me know if there is anything we can do to help you." He turned to go but Cobra called back.

"Actually, there is one other thing." He turned politely, waiting for her to continue. "We suspect that someone other than Vago is planning to attack, and I know you have families all over Lasina. If you should hear anything, would you send word?"

"Absolutely, I can't wait for peace to be here, in this land again," He spoke softly, before turning back and shrinking back down, the tentacle disappearing into the depths.

"Now, that is a man to admire," Cobra spoke, and I looked oddly at her. "Not the King, Harvey, the Kraken."

"What? That's a man?" I asked, thinking it had been an animal.

"Yes, what did you think he was? He was orphaned as a child and the Nymphs raised him. He chooses to spend all his time in that form with his adopted family." We walked towards the trees as she spoke. She bent down to place a tiny home on the ground, before walking back towards her own cabin and placing the second one down. She used her magic to grow them to the full size. "I think this will do. Evat and Escu can have that one and Jeca can have this one." I smiled as I noticed Jeca's was closer to her own cabin.

"Do you think they will like them?" I asked, as we began walking back towards the castle.

"The real question is, do you really want them living with you and your men?" She laughed as I stumbled over my feet. "I didn't think so."

"I hadn't thought about that. Let's get them settled, so I can have peace." We walked back slowly, even though I was itching for Evat, Escu, and Jeca to be out of the castle.

By the time everyone was settled into their new homes and the sun was setting, a new disturbance filled the entryway. All I could hear was swearing and the guards wrestling with someone. I heard Viper's voice speaking an odd language, then silence. Sic was the first one down the stairs and he barked for the guards to let the man go, but they refused.

"Why did you bring Rizhaq here? Why are the guards pinning him down?" Sic pushed one of the guards aside until Viper stepped in front of him.

"He is the one who hired me to kill Jeca." I watched as Sic's face paled and he looked at the man on the floor.

"Thuzo!" He yelled, and the man came running. "I want him placed in the dungeons and I want you to personally watch over him until morning. You may tell Sage I'm sorry, but I need answers from him, and I don't want him dying before I get them," Sic commanded, and Viper stepped closer and whispered something to Sic. He nodded, and she followed Thuzo and the guards out the door.

"What did she ask?" I said, when I reached his side.

"She asked if she could keep watch as well." I looked at his face and it was hard but some of the color had returned.

"Do you know that man, Sic?" I couldn't push away the sensation that he did, and that is why he reacted the way he had.

"He is my mother's personal servant." I couldn't hold the pearl clutching gasp back and he sighed. "I've suspected that she wasn't happy with things, but I don't see why she would attack another King." He turned and walked up the stairs without another word. Emot reached my side and tugged me up them as well.

23

Maisie

Emot said good night to me as we got into the room. Zugo stood by his door for a moment. "Sweet dreams, Maisie," He said, before pecking me on the lips and walking towards the sitting room. I remembered that it was his night to keep watch, but I wasn't tired.

All the excitement of the day wouldn't let my mind sit still so I walked into the bathroom to grab my robe. I stripped my clothes off, as I pulled the robe around me and tied it. I walked out to the bedroom and heard things smashing in Sic's room, as Emot stood in his doorway listening. I was about to go to Sic when Emot shook his head no.

"Is he going to be alright?" I asked, and he smiled.

"He will be fine, Kai is in there, and they are most likely sparring." I heard a thud on the wall and a grunt of pain. "Sic and Kai like to box, usually in the courtyard." Emot walked over to me and pulled me close. "I love you, Maisie. I don't know if I've told you that recently."

He pressed his lips to mine prompting my own whisper, "I love you too, Emot." His second kiss was harder, and he began to pull me towards his room, but I stopped him. "Not tonight, I

haven't spent much time with Zugo, and Sic is obviously not going to be wanting my attention for a while, so," I trailed off, not wanting to hurt his feelings.

"I understand, we all have to share." I kissed him once more and turned to walk out to the sitting room. "I'll leave the door open in case you want to come in later." I laughed at his hopeful offer and slipped out the door, closing it softly behind me.

Zugo looked up from a book, as he sat in the window seat and smiled at me. "Do you mind if I sit with you for a bit?"

"Not at all." He smiled and closed the book, placing it on the seat next to him.

"What were you reading?" I tried to get a look and he slid it under him more. His skin turned red, prompting me to scoot closer to try to grab it.

"It's a novel Sic gave to me. He gave me a bunch of things to read and this one seemed interesting." He held it up and I read the title.

"It's an erotica?" My question was more about the novel than him reading it.

"I think so. There are some very interesting scenes in here, and a few very..." he trailed off for a moment, "Detailed scenes."

"Hmm, any you want to try?" I teased, and he looked at me more closely.

"Well, a few, but that will have to wait until later. But there has been one thing that I was going to ask you about," His words stopped and stuttered slightly, so I smiled reassuringly.

"We already talked about this. You can ask for anything, or say anything." He smiled and then looked me straight in the eyes.

"The other night you sucked on me, and I know Sic was doing much the same to you but how? Like, how does he do it?" He blushed as he asked about eating pussy, and my heart melted.

"You know how we kissed with our tongues?" He nodded in response to my inquiry. "Well, you do that, only down there, and you use your tongue to rub my clit." His eyes got wider, and I almost knew the next question he was going to ask, but he didn't.

He looked out the window for a moment, thinking things over and then asked, "Can I try that?" I smiled, nodding.

"Do you want to do it now?" I asked and he blushed more.

"I guess not right this second, that isn't very romantic." He picked up the book again and I was wondering if he was going to go back to reading, when he opened it to a page and handed it to me. "I wanna try this, one day."

I began to read the page and looked back at Zugo for a second, before continuing. The scene was one with a woman using a dildo on a guy, and I was intrigued by his choice. I didn't think it was about the dildo per say, but her domination of the man that was exciting to him. "Do you want me to use the dildo or dominate you?" This definitely required clarification.

"I think..." he trailed off, and I saw him fidget in his seat. "Maybe both? I don't want one of the guys doing it, but I kinda wanna have you do it." So, he wanted to be the submissive Now, that excited me.

"Okay." I tapped my finger on my lip and thought for a moment. "Stand up." He stood up and tossed the book onto the seat. "Now kneel." He lowered himself to his knees and I stepped closer to him.

"I want to see you play with your cocks." I made this a bit softer and he scrambled to open his pants for me. Once both cocks sprang free, he stroked himself slowly. I walked over to the couch and sat down, watching him work himself. "Slower."

He slowed his hands so that they snailed their way up and down. I loosened the tie of my robe and opened it wide, exposing my body to him. His gaze devoured my flesh, and his cocks jumped in excitement. "Come closer, but stay on your knees." He crawled forward until I stopped him with my foot. He faced me fully as I slid one finger down my slit, before bringing it to my lips to lick it.

His eyes widened as he watched me slide my finger into my mouth before returning it to my slit. He kept his pace slow as I teased him with the view, his eyes devouring my movements. "Come, eat my pussy." Removing my fingers, I watched him hesitate for a moment, then spoke again. "I said. COME. EAT. MY. PUSSY," My voice was soft but firm, and he crawled closer on his knees. His eyes locked on mine as he bent forward and tentatively licked me.

He closed his eyes and then he swirled his tongue around my clit. I reached down to slide my fingers through his hair, burying him just a bit more between my legs. "Pretend you're licking your plate clean," I instructed, and his mouth opened more so he could lick my entire slit. Once he got the hang of it, I stopped instructing him and let him go at his own pace. I watched as his hand still slid up and down his cocks while he feasted.

I leaned my head back as he got into the groove and noticed Emot standing over me, watching him work. He had a shit eating grin on his face, as he enjoyed the show Zugo and I were putting on. He lifted his finger to his lips before sliding his hands into his pockets. My eyes drifted closed for a moment trying to enjoy Zugo's movements, but it wasn't enough. This seriously sucked in terms of having to teach Zugo what to do, and at this point, I was just getting frustrated.

"Want some pointersss?" Emot asked, causing Zugo to freeze. My eyes snapped open and noticed that Zugo was comically sitting there with his tongue half out. His eyes were locked on Emot with a deer in the headlights look, making Emot snort. "Ssshe isssn't going to break, firssst off, sssecond, ssshe isssn't going to get off if you don't add more pressssure. Pretend that ssshe isss a meal and you're sssstarving to death, get up in there."

Emot walked around the couch and sat on the window seat, out of the way. "I'm jussst here for the ssshow." I pulled Zugo's face back around to face me and looked at my pussy and then his mouth, signaling with my eyes for him to go again. He stopped stroking himself and slid his hands onto my knees, pushing them wider open. This time, when his mouth touched me, it was glorious.

He buried his face and licked harder, teasing my clit before sliding his tongue into me. My eyes closed again, enjoying this more, now that he seemed to get the pointers Emot gave him. I twisted my fingers into his hair again, before moaning as he hit a good spot. He repeated the action making me moan even more, then I felt his fingers swirling around my slit. Gently, he pressed one in, then two, stroking me as he sucked hard on my clit.

My noises became louder and I opened my eyes to look at him. His eyes were closed, as in if pleasure, and I noticed Emot on

the window seat, stoking his cocks as he watched. Zugo added another finger just then and I shattered without warning. He groaned against my clit as I moaned loudly, while my body clamped onto his fingers. When I opened my eyes once more, he was gazing at me with a proud look on his face, his fingers still buried in my folds.

"Did I tell you that you could stop?" I said, and he instantly buried his face back into my pussy, picking up where he left off.

Emot rose from the window seat and slid onto the couch next to me. "Godsss, I wanna fuck you while he eatsss your pussssy," He whispered into my ear, but didn't try to get any closer. "Want me to sssuck him while he eatsss you?" Emot asked loud enough for Zugo to hear, and Zugo's eye snapped open to look at me. I could see the indecision in his gaze, wanting his own release but not sure if he wanted Emot to do it.

"I think he might enjoy that," I said, before commanding Zugo to shift his cocks together. Emot let the gravity pull him off the couch and onto the floor beside Zugo, then laid down so his head was under Zugo's chest.

"The view from down here isss even better," He said, then Zugo moaned into my clit as he added a fourth finger. His speed increased and I could tell Emot was sucking him hard, because Zugo worked me just as hard. It didn't take long for my body to climb that peak once again and I flooded Zugo's face as I cried out. He groaned as he continued, but I pushed him back so I could watch Emot suck his cock.

Zugo looked down to watch while sucking the fingers he had used on me. Emot sucked harder making Zugo's head fall back. I rose and walked behind Zugo and knelt, sliding my hands up under his shirt. "I want you to fill Emot's throat with cum," I hissed in his ear, and he shivered in my arms. Running my nails

down his back, he moaned at my rough treatment. I pushed him forward slightly and swirled a finger around his ass. Pressing ever so softly, I let the tip of my finger breach him. He pressed back slightly, and I began to move my finger.

Emot was still stroking himself while sucking Zugo and I fingered his ass. "Do you want two?" I asked, causing him to moan a yes. Slowly, I worked a second finger in beside the first. Within about five strokes, I heard him groan and felt him cum. "That's it, give Emot all that cum." Emot swallowed him down as his own cocks spasmed and shot cum up his shirt. Pulling my hand back, Zugo leaned back against me as Emot licked his tip like an ice cream before sitting up.

Emot swiped his thumb over his bottom lip as he stood, and without a word walked back into the room. Zugo slowly turned and pulled me close to his chest. We cuddled on the floor for a few minutes until he sighed. "Are you alright?" I asked, and he smiled.

"Yeah, that was just intense." He pulled me into his lap covering me with my robe, so I was cozy and warm. "Definitely want to try it again." I snuggled up in his arms and hummed my agreement as he rubbed my back.

"Just wait till we have sex," I murmured, as I began to relax into his embrace. He kissed my head in answer and then I fell asleep.

Zugo

Maisie fell asleep in my arms and I couldn't have been happier. Emot came back after she was already sleeping, and sat on the couch. I noticed he had changed into a robe. "Want to take her to bed? Or I can, if you don't want to." Slowly rising, I carried Maisie to her bed and tucked her in.

Returning to the sitting room, I grabbed my book off the window seat and sat in the chair. "Can I ask you a question?" I hesitated, but was beyond curious.

"Ssshoot. I got nowhere elssse to be." Emot leaned back and propped his feet up on the couch.

"What does it feel like?" I asked, and he looked at me like he didn't understand.

"You're gonna have to clarify. Do you wanna know what pussssy feelsss like, what assss feelsss like, what it feelsss like to take a dick in your assss, or sssucking a dick... I mean you gotta ssspecify here. You know what it feels like to eat pussssy, so I'll ssskip that one." He chuckled and I realized I kind of wanted to know it all.

"All of it, I guess, but definitely the first one," I mumbled, and he looked up for a moment.

"Ssso, you know how if feelsss when she sssuckssd your dick, or me... It'sss kinda like that, only hotter and tighter. When ssshe cumsss, her body ssstartsss to sssqueeze tighter, over and over." His eyes had drifted shut as he described it. "It'sss sssslippery, and when you cum it feelsss like heaven." He shook his head as he opened his eyes. "Sssorry."

"No, I get it, I think. I guess I'm just nervous," I said, making him smile.

"Don't be. Jussst take your time, and ssshe might not get off the firssst time, but then again, ssshe might, and remember, ssshe won't break. The table might, but ssshe won't." He laughed at that, and I remembered Sic's desk collapsing.

"Okay, so what about the other stuff?" I hesitated to name it all.

"Assss is much the sssame asss pusssy, at leassst when you're giving it. Taking a dick up the assss is intenssse. It'sss hard to dessscribe, like ssstretching but in a pleasssurable way, and then when it movesss it rubsss placesss you didn't even realize you had. Orgasmsss are more intensssse, too, and when they cum, it feelsss amazing. That'sss about all I can sssay on that. Did you like her fingersss in your assss?" He asked, and I blushed, not realizing he had noticed.

"It felt good, yes," I blushed harder, as I admitted it to him.

"Well, there ya go. Asss far asss sssucking dick goesss, that'sss a persssonal thing. Persssonally, I love it. That'sss one where you won't know till you try, although, cum is ssssalty, but I

like the tassste." He knit his hands together behind his head and closed his eyes. "Anything elssse you wanna know?"

"Does a dildo feel the same as a cock?" I whispered, and he cracked an eye.

"It'sss sssimilar, but not as pliable as a real cock ssso you have to be careful about how hard you go with it. I think we might have one around here sssomewhere," He closed his eyes again, as he spoke.

My mind pondered everything he had said and there was only one thing I wanted to ask, but kinda wanted to wait. "Does Maisie like watching you with the others?" I changed gears to get my mind off it.

He sighed softly and smiled. "When we were on the boat, coming to get you, Sssic and Kai were fucking while I fucked Maisssie. The more ssshe could see the wetter ssshe got. I think it'sss sssafe to sssay ssshe likesss to watch. Then again, so do I, one of thessse daysss I'll get a video camera from Earth and make a movie of you guysss fucking her."

"What's a video?" I asked, and he sat up. Picking up an odd device off the side table, he clicked a button and the picture over the fireplace slid up. The black screen behind it flickered to life and Emot stood to put a disk into a small box.

"Thisss isss a video," He said, as images began to flash on the screen.

"Okay, that is cool," I said, as I moved from the chair to the couch.

"Thisss isss a good movie. we don't have channelsss like Earth doesss, but we bought a fuck ton of moviesss and can

alwaysss go get more." He sat next to me as the movie began to play and we both became silent as the action started. We spent the rest of the night watching movies, without talking.

Maisie

I slept late the next morning and woke to find Sic sitting on the side of my bed smiling. "Good morning," He said softly, and I stretched while yawning.

"Good morning. Have you been here long?" I asked, and he smiled as he stood.

"Actually, no, I saw you stirring, so I've been here about a minute, but since you are up, we need to question Rizhaq today, and I would like for you to be there." He watched as I tossed the covers aside and stood up on top of the bed. Without thinking, I jumped at him and he caught me, kissing me before putting me on the floor. "Go get dressed."

He slapped my ass as I walked off towards the bathroom. I washed my face and brushed my teeth before dropping my robe on the floor and walking to my closet. Kai whistled as I walked by, but kept walking towards the sitting room. I tossed a dress on, just because I was being lazy, and it was easy, then I left the room. Sic was waiting for me in the sitting area, as Emot and Zugo slept on the couch.

"Why are they out here?" I asked as I walked past on tiptoe, and the guards closed the door behind us.

"They were up all-night watching TV. I think it was Zugo's first movie fest," Sic explained, as we walked down the stairs. "Thuzo and Viper are waiting for us and we can fill in the other two later."

Kai and Jeca were waiting for us outside the barracks, following us in as we opened the doors. "Do you think he will talk?" Jeca asked, as we walked down the steps.

"He better, or his death will not be quick," Sic said, and I shivered at the menace I heard in his voice.

Viper was leaning against the bars about halfway down the long hallway, while Thuzo yawned. "You may go, Thuzo, thank you for personally watching over him."

"No trouble, Your Highness. He hasn't spoken at all." Thuzo walked off and Viper snorted.

"That's because he was spelled to keep quiet," She whispered something I didn't catch, and Rizhaq instantly began blubbering. "Feel like talking Rizhaq?" She hissed, and walked closer to the bars.

He shied back away from her and begged Sic to let him free, that she was wrong, and he was innocent. "They always say that, don't they?" Kai said, as he fished a key from his pocket. Opening the door, he grabbed Rizhaq by the back of the neck and pulled him out of the cell. Pushing him deeper into the dungeon, he shoved him into a windowless room and then hit a switch on the wall.

The room was painted white, of all things, and in the middle of the room was a chair with a drain under it. "Oh, I'm going to have so much fun in here." Viper rubbed her hands together as Kai forced Rizhaq into the chair and strapped him in.

172

"Let's see, what should we start with?" She perused the tables lined with all sorts of instruments. Jeca picked up a pair of pliers and handed them to her. She smiled and clamped them together while turning towards Rizhaq.

I paled as I realized her intentions and so did Rizhaq. "Answer the questions correctly and truthfully, or this is going to be a very bad day," Viper hissed, and Sic looked at me.

He pulled me out of the room and sat me in a chair off to the side. "You don't have to stay if you don't want to." I nodded but stayed outside of the room, choosing not to watch, but I needed to hear what he was saying.

"Let's start with an easy one, shall we?" Viper's words could easily be heard from the hallway, and I was thankful I wouldn't have to watch. "Who do you work for?"

"My mistress is Queen Salima Wells," He answered with a touch of fear in his voice.

"Did you hire me to kill Jeca Harding?" She asked simply, but I didn't hear him answer.

The sound of screaming reached my ears, but then Rizhaq screamed a 'Yes'. "Were you the one to devise the scheme?" Jeca's voice sounded deadly in the quiet.

"No," I heard Rizhaq's quick answer.

"Who told you to hire an assassin to kill me?" His voice rose slightly, his anger showing no doubt. Once again, I heard screaming and cringed as something popped loudly in the room.

"Salima told me to hire her," Rizhaq's voice was hoarse, and I cringed when I realized the implications of Sic's mother trying to kill Kai's father.

I rose from the chair, squared my shoulders and marched into the room. Sic tried to shield me from seeing Rizhaq but I pushed past him. "Why?" I was pissed, and frankly, he deserved to die, but I wanted answers now.

He tried to garner pity from me, but I held out my hand towards Viper and she placed the pliers in my palm. "Don't think I won't use them. You attempted to have a King of Lasina killed. NOW, WHY?" I was yelling by the time I finished speaking, and Rizhaq shrank back in the chair. My basilisk pushed forward, and I could smell his fear.

"She intends to attack the Southern Kingdom," He admitted softly. "She thought it would be easier if Jeca was out of the way."

Sic stepped up next to me before asking, "Why would she attack the Southern Kingdom?"

Rizhaq seemed resigned to answer our questions at this point, and he began to tell us everything. "She has been working with Vago to rule all of Lasina. She said that the treaty should have never been forced on you and that she would kill anyone who stood in her way to getting you out of it." Sic ran a hand through his hair and walked back towards the door.

But Rizhaq wasn't done spilling the beans yet, "She hired an assassin to scare Her Majesty, then another to steal a bloody shirt." That made me realize that he was speaking about my shirt.

"Do you mean my shirt?" I asked, and he nodded. "Why would she need my shirt?"

"She used it to trick your mother, she planned on telling your mother you were dead, so she wouldn't come back to Lasina. But your mother didn't believe her, and they fought. Salima came back from Earth all bloody and said that Clara would never be a problem again," He spoke, and the room began to spin. I dropped the pliers to the floor with a loud clattering as I began to sink.

Kai was the one who caught me before I fell, and he carried me out of the room. "Take her upstairs," Sic's words were kind, and he brushed a lock of hair off my face before Kai carried me out of the dungeon.

"I'm sorry, Maisie," He spoke, but I barely heard his words. The realization that Sic's mother had killed mine, broke the dam I had erected on my feelings and I turned my head into Kai's shoulder and bawled.

Kai let me get all my tears out as he held me tightly in his arms. I heard Emot and Zugo for a moment, but Kai shushed them as he laid me in bed. "Just rest here for a bit and I'll come back in soon." I heard him leave the room and cried into my pillow harder.

By the time my tears stopped, Emot and Zugo had been filled in on what Rizhaq had said. Sic was still gone, but Kai had returned and told me that Rizhaq had told them all about Salima and much more. It turned out that she had killed Sic's father a few years ago, and she had been sleeping with Vago for quite some time. She was also the reason Vago had come to Earth, when we had been forced to flee.

It turns out she was the mysterious woman I had seen with Vago the day that he had taken me. With most of her deeds now out in the open, I worried about what she would do next. Kai

assured me that whatever it was, she wouldn't get her hands on me.

After dark, Sic returned to the room covered in grime and walked straight into his room, closing the door behind him. Emot walked in there to see what had happened. Kai told me that Viper and Jeca had killed Rizhaq after all his secrets had been revealed, and then buried him. Thankfully, he didn't go into any more details.

Emot stumbled out of Sic's room and leaned against the wall. His face was pale and instantly, I knew something was wrong. "What happened?" I asked, as I rushed over to where he had slid down the wall, to sit on the floor.

I knelt down in front of him and his eyes looked hurt, almost as if he wanted to cry himself. "He's leaving. He said he was going to shower and then he was going to leave." Emot's words were like a knife to the heart and I rose. I walked into Sic's room prepared for a battle.

The shower was still on when I marched into Sic's room, slamming the door behind me. I walked into the bathroom and opened the shower door. Sic turned just as I stepped in, fully dressed, and pushed him against the tile. "You are not leaving," I ignored the water soaking my dress, as I spoke.

He looked me dead in the eye then whispered, "It's safer for everyone if I leave."

I poked him in the chest several times before wiping the water from my face angrily. "You listen here, Sicrin Wells. YOU. ARE. NOT. LEAVING." I emphasized my words with pokes to his chest.

He reached up and turned the water off while I wiped my face. "My mother killed yours, or have you forgotten that?"

I shook my head at him. "You aren't your mother," My voice was sad, and I turned to step out of the shower.

He grabbed my arm to stop me. "Could you live with it? Could you honestly tell me that what my mother did doesn't color how you see me? It sure as fuck changes how I see myself." He released his grip and I stepped out of the shower as he followed.

My dress was soaked and plastered to my body, but I didn't care. Crossing my arms over my chest, I looked at him. "If you leave, you're not just hurting me. Emot loves you. I love you. Why would you throw that all away?" I shivered in the cool air watching Sic drip on the floor. "And yes, I can live with it, because you are not her."

"Her actions taint me; they taint my brothers and the whole of the Western Kingdom. I can't just ignore what she has done," I could hear the pain in his voice.

"Sic, you are good and kind. Your first thought isn't about power, but about me and my safety. You are NOTHING like her," I tried to speak firmly but I could hear the chattering of my teeth.

He pulled a towel off the counter and wrapped it around my shoulders, not bothering to dry himself off. "If she plans to attack the Southern Kingdom and me leaving will stop her, then I have to leave." He walked to a small closet and grabbed another towel to dry off with.

He wrapped it around his waist and walked towards his bedroom. I followed him slowly, digesting what he had said. "What makes you think you leaving will stop her? You heard what he said, she's been sleeping with Vago. For all we know, they planned this together," He sat on the edge of the bed, as I spoke.

"Who knows what she would do, but I have to try to stop her," He argued, and the door slammed against the wall hard, making me jump. Cobra stood there, her eyes clouded over, Viper stood just behind her with the same clouded expression. While we watched, they clasped hands and the two merged into one being. I gaped as they began to speak, the duel voices echoing around the room.

"Sicrin Wells, you cannot leave,

for if you do, this land will grieve.

The Queen has planned, the price is paid,

for her deeds, she shall be flayed.

The love that stands within your sight,

will not part without a fight.

Take the course time has woven,

and see to those that you have chosen.

Disregard us at your will,

but if you do, her blood will spill."

They both pointed in my direction before they split back apart, and their eyes cleared. Cobra looked at both of us and then walked out without another word. Viper, on the other hand, shook her head. "You're a fool if you think leaving is the right choice." Then she grabbed the door and walked out, slamming it closed behind her.

Shocked, I stood looking at the wooden panel that they had exited through. I could feel my dress dripping onto my feet as a chill ran over my skin. "Were they just...?" I asked, pointing my fingers every which way trying to explain.

"Yes. They are what is called Astrozygotic Twins. They actually live on two separate planes of existence. They are two sides to a whole, neither can have children without the other, neither can fully love without the other. There have only been three cases of them in history," Sic explained from behind me, and I turned to look at him.

"How do you know all this?" I asked in awe.

"I enjoy reading, anything really, but history is definitely my favorite subject. I also read several medical books while learning to use my healing abilities." He looked at me softly and smiled. Switching topics swiftly, I looked him in the eyes before I began to pace.

"Where was I before they came in?" I shook my head to clear it and remembered. "Now I remember, what if this is all their plan, and regardless of you leaving or not, they do it?"

"You heard what they said, right? If I leave, you die, even if I hated you, I couldn't put you at risk like that. And I don't, hate you, that is. I love you." Sic ran a hand through his hair in frustration. "What are we going to do?"

"Well we need to plan. How will we help the people in the Southern Kingdom? We can't move them here since we are out of room at the moment. As soon as there is peace, I am kicking everyone out to their own lands again, they can keep the houses if they want." Sic laughed at my words while standing, his towel falling to the floor, and I was sidetracked for the moment by the view of his skin.

"We also need to figure out how to get my father to stop attacking the Eastern Kingdom. Emot might have some ideas about that, I'll go get him, and Zugo and Kai too, they can help us plan." I turned towards the door only to have Sic stop me.

"You are adorable when you're worked up." He kissed my shoulder and I sighed. "First, we need to get you dry, before you get Sic," He hissed softly, and I shuddered.

"Did you just make a pun using your own name?" I asked trying to distract him, while secretly hoping it failed. We had been shooting sparks for days now, and I desperately needed to burn.

"I did. Now shut up and be a good girl, or I'll tie you up again." He pulled the towel from my body and dropped it to the floor. Skimming his hands down my body, he hiked up my dress and pulled it over my head. Tossing ts aside, I turned to look up at him.

"Sic, if you aren't going to take this all the way, I don't think I can stand it. And if you do and then leave..." I trailed off not wanting to finish my sentence.

"I won't leave, I promise." He tipped my chin up and placed a soft kiss on my lips before picking me up and carrying me to the bed.

Sic laid me in the center of his bed and reached between the headboard and mattress to pull a ball gag out. "Open up, honey." I tentatively opened my mouth so he could slide the gag between my lips. He fastened the buckle and then grinned devilishly. "We can't have you screaming too loud. I'm going to make you beg me to stop because of too much pleasure."

He crawled onto the bed, sliding up my body with his. I could feel his cocks, but he didn't dive right in. Instead, he slithered down my body, until his head was between my thighs. He looked up at me and hissed, his eyes changing to his basilisk's eyes. He flicked his forked tongue out and trailed it up my inner thigh, all the while looking up to keep my gaze. Repeating the action with my other thigh had me shifting them wider in invitation. His tongue dipped into my belly button then trailed down to the very top of my clit before he sucked it back in.

"I can sssmell your desssire, tassste you on the air," He hissed again, as he flicked his tongue out again, this time circling my outer lips but not giving me enough stimulation. He drew lazy shapes all around my pussy, never touching where I ached the most. I writhed on the bed as he teased my flesh with just the tips of his tongue.

I desperately wanted him to touch my clit with his tongue, and when he finally did, I cried out in pleasure, my voice muffled by the gag. He flicked his tongue up and down my clit, never giving enough pressure to send me over the edge. His hands slid up my thighs until his finger teased my slit, never entering. He began to press a bit more firmly and then his fingers began to open my slit. His fingers still didn't slide in and I thrashed to get more friction.

Flicking harder, he set me off and I screamed around the gag as I spasmed. The second I began to cum, Sic slid his tongue deep, sending me even higher. He never stopped and his thumb worked my clit as his tongue fucked me. I was barely able to catch my breath before a second orgasm flooded my system with pleasure. All I could do was mewl in pleasure as I came.

Sic rose onto his knees and pulled his tongue from between my legs as he stroked himself. He shifted his cocks into one so slowly, I silently begged him to rush. If he was going to 'just the tip' it again, I was gonna hit him with something, hard. He stroked himself while I watched, then positioned the head of his cock just at my entrance.

He didn't slide in as expected but let just the head of his cock part my folds, over and over. The friction rubbed my clit, but I wanted him deep. I wiggled to try and get him deeper, but he just pinned my hips to the bed. "If you're going to be a naughty girl, I'll tie you to thisss bed," His words made me wetter, and he slid in just a fraction deeper.

"I want you to cum all over thisss cock, like a good girl," He hissed, as he watched the head of his cock part me just a little. He slipped in a fraction more and began to hit my g-spot just a bit.

"More," I tried to say around the gag, but it came out muffled.

184

"No, no, no. You will cum before you get more." I guess he had understood me. His thumb slid over my clit once and I begged for more. My body tightened as he sped up a tiny bit, but he never went further in. By the time he had me thrashing again I could feel my juices coating his cock. "Cum on this cock," He said, and I shattered screaming as I flooded him. He buried his cock deep in my body as I came, and my scream turned into a louder moan.

He didn't move at first, just held still and waited for my body to adjust and relax around him. My spasms faded completely before he leaned down onto his elbows and kissed my face. His gentle kisses began to match his long slow movements, and I could feel him pull almost all the way out before sliding back in. I moaned as he worked my body slowly, then I felt the latch to the ball gag release as he pulled it free.

His lips claimed mine as he slowly sped up the pace until I could do nothing but hold on to him. Wrapping my legs around his waist so he hit all my nerves, he swallowed my moan as I orgasmed around him again. Leaning back, he pulled me astride his lap and lifted me on and off him. He swung his legs out from under him, and slowly laid back.

He left me sitting on top of him. "Ride me, honey, hard and fast." His hands left my body and he put his hands behind his head, just watching my tits bounce as I rode. I did as he commanded and rode him hard and fast until I felt my body begin to tighten again. "Play with your tits," He commanded, and my hands slid up to my breasts. Massaging them for a moment, I pinched my nipples as Sic pinched my clit and I threw my head back. He repeated the action and I whimpered as another orgasm swept over me.

I collapsed onto his chest, but he didn't stop. "I told you, I'm not stopping until you beg me too, we can go for the next two days if that's what it takes, but you will beg."

He lifted his legs and rocked into me, his movements back to slow once more. His hands grabbed my waist and rolled my hips, so he rubbed my clit more and I cried out with each thrust. By the time my body clamped around his, I was begging for him to stop. My begging sent his own body over the edge and I felt his cock fill me with hot cum. My body locked down on his making him groan louder as he came again.

We were both breathing rapidly, and his heart was racing as we laid locked together. "Could you really go for two days?" I asked, and he laughed.

"Probably not, but I damn sure would have tried if that is what it took." I giggled and put my chin on his chest so I could look up at him. "I love you, Maisie."

"I love you too, Sic." I felt my body slowly release his but neither of us wanted to move, so I laid my head back on his chest. He rubbed my back until we both dozed off.

I heard whispers and peeked my eyes open. The first thing I noticed was Emot standing over the foot of the bed looking at Sic. Sic's voice was just as soft as his, but I shifted, and he knew I was awake. I slowly sat up realizing that Sic was still hard inside me.

I crawled off his cock and rolled over to look up at Emot. He smiled and tilted his head. "Hello love, sssleep well?" Nodding my head, I rolled once more and climbed out and ran to the bathroom. Emot chuckled as I heard the bed creak, but my

bladder was more important. After I flushed and washed my hands, I walked back out of the bathroom.

Sic was sitting up next to Emot on the foot of the bed, Emot's hands in Sic hair as they kissed. I decided to give them some alone time and began tiptoeing towards the door when Sic's voice stopped me, "Where do you think you're going?" Turning on my heels, I noticed both of them staring at me as if I was a meal they wanted to eat.

"I just thought you might want to be alone for a bit, that's all," Emot rose as I spoke, and walked towards the door. I thought he was about to leave and then I heard the lock engage. Looking over my shoulder, I watched as he peeled his shirt off and tossed it aside, his pants followed swiftly.

He slid up behind me and wrapped his arms around my waist. "I think thisss isss going to be a game for three." He turned me in his arms before dropping low and tossing me over his shoulder. As I hung there, I had a perfect view of his ass, while he walked back towards the bed.

He laid me down next to Sic and then climbed over me. "What ssshould we do with our naughty girl?" Emot asked Sic, as he sat across my hips.

"I don't know, but she does enjoy watching almost as much as she enjoys riding. Maybe we give her a show." Sic pulled Emot off me and pulled him in for another kiss. This one was fierce, and my body responded instantly as Sic began to stroke Emot's cocks. I wiggled back towards the headboard when Sic's hand grabbed my ankle and they both looked at me like I was next. "Hmm, Emot, I think we need to tie up our little escape artist. What do you think?"

"I agree, but I don't think the bed will give her the best view of the ssshow, do you?" Emot's words made me shiver about the same time as Sic's hand slid up my leg and teased my folds softly with a finger, keeping me from moving with his skilled hands. Emot's fingers caressed my breasts and tweaked my nipples. Sic crawled over me and pressed his lips to mine, softly tangling his tongue with mine.

When he broke the kiss, he looked me in the eyes and asked. "Are you going to be a good girl?" I dazedly shook my head yes and he grinned. "Good, now on your knees." His fingers didn't stop teasing me as I scrambled onto my knees.

Emot pulled me to face him and wrapped my hands around the base of both cocks. "I think she needs to be nice and wet before we give her a show. Emot what do you think?" Sic's fingers slid between my folds as he spoke, and he began stroking me.

Emot's hand caressed my body until two of his fingers joined Sic's. "I fully agree," Was all he said, as they stroked my body together. My body instantly responded to them both and they worked me till I was dripping, but deliberately left me wanting more. Sic pulled his hand free and then crawled behind Emot. Emot laid down and rolled so his face was between my thighs and Sic used my wetness to lube his cock up.

I watched as Sic lined himself up and slid deep into Emot. I felt Emot spread my legs more and then his tongue joined his fingers, and I moaned. Sic began to work Emot hard while I devoured the sight, Emot mimicking Sic's movements with his tongue. Emot's cocks combined and Sic bent me forward so I could see more, but also so I could suck Emot's cock.

Emot moaned as I took him into my mouth and sent vibrations through my pussy. I moaned around him as Sic picked up speed and the pace became more frantic. We all rushed

towards a sweet release and I broke first, flooding Emot's mouth as I came on his face. That sent him off and I felt his cock pulse before hot cum shot down my throat. Sic slammed into Emot a few more times and then groaned as his own orgasm hit.

I collapsed off to the side while Sic fell forward onto Emot. My body was fully relaxed, but my stomach growled suddenly. Emot was kissing Sic, so I slipped from bed and began walking towards the door. "I'll be there in a moment," Emot called, but his voice was cut off by Sic.

"Just going to get something to eat, I'll be fine by myself," I called back, as Sic began to move over Emot again. I unlocked the door and slipped out. I took one last look at the pleasure on Emot's face as I closed the door.

28

Emot

Sic kept me in bed for two hours, making me cum over and over before he finally came again. Maisie had left and hadn't returned, giving Sic and me some time alone. I needed to reassure myself that he wasn't leaving. Sic was still buried in my body as we cuddled, and I was dreamily enjoying the connectedness I felt. As we cuddled, a knock sounded on the bedroom door before it opened a bit.

Zugo's face peered around the wood and he looked up as Sic sat up slightly. "Um... sorry to bother you, but an emissary has arrived from the Nymphs." His eyes grew larger when Sic pulled out and rose, pulling me up as well.

"We will be right there." Sic walked to his closet, tossing my clothes to me as he passed them. I threw my clothes on and walked towards the door. Zugo backed away as I opened it fully and saw Kai standing there with a grin.

"Have fun you two?" I rolled my eyes at his question.

"Where's Maisie?" Sic asked as he joined us, pulling a shirt over his head.

"She was in the kitchens when they arrived," Kai said with a bit of a pissed look on his face. "Naked," He added, and my eyebrows rose.

"Well, she greeted them as they naturally are," Sic said, as we began to walk out the bedroom and towards the stairs. "So, I doubt they will care."

"Oh, they didn't. But I don't know how much I want other men to look at Maisie's naked body," Kai spoke possessively, and I kind of agreed. "I mean if I could, I would keep her naked and screaming at all hours of the day, but other than you three, I don't want men looking at her."

I rolled my eyes as I began to hear Maisie's voice from the great hall. We turned the corner and I saw Maisie sitting in a chair, gloriously naked and speaking with two men, one clearly from the water Nymphs the other decidedly not. "Here they are." She rose and both men rose as well, each just as naked as Maisie. Both Nymphs bowed and then I noticed the other Nymph's horns peaking from his hair.

"We are sorry to disturb you so late at night, but Cobra and Her Majesty told us that if anything occurred, we were to come directly to you," The water Nymph spoke, as Sic held out his hand.

"May we please sit?" Maisie sat slowly and we all joined her at the table. "This is Solise from the Water Nymphs, and this is Opysis from the Wood Nymphs that lived in the Eastern Kingdom. The King of the Wood Nymphs is requesting sanctuary here within our walls. I would like to offer them that, but we are having difficulties determining where they should be located," Maisie introduced us to the men, and Sic was the first to speak up.

"Are you at your full size, or have you grown for the purposes of this meeting?" He asked Opysis.

"This is not my normal size, Your Majesty. We are just not as small as the water Nymphs, we stand about two feet tall," Opysis answered good naturedly. "Another reason why we are having trouble with the location. However, we are vastly smaller than the Water Kingdom in terms of population, we breed very rarely so our numbers are smaller."

"Are you able to live near the Gryphons?" Sic asked suddenly, and I realized the mountain pasture would be a great place for them.

"What about the pasture near the Gryphons? That way they aren't encroaching on the Gryphons' territory, but there is plenty of space near the woods there." Maisie smiled at me and I desperately wanted to be alone with her.

"That is a wonderful idea, you two. If you want, when the sun comes up, we can have Cobra add walls to include the mountains as well, giving you added protection. Would you need homes provided by us? I will be honest I have no idea how you live," She admitted, taking the reins again. My cocks stiffened as she easily slid into the role of the Queen, looking out for all the innocent victims of her father's terror.

"We will gladly build our own homes. we have magical abilities that will easily accomplish that task. Walls, however, would be greatly appreciated," Just as he spoke, Cobra walked into the great hall.

"Pardon my intrusion, but I wanted to let you know that the walls have already been placed around the mountain pasture and a large gate has been added to the mountain pass. I would suggest we get these Wood Nymphs settled quickly. more will be

arriving soon." Cobra eyed the Nymphs and Maisie before turning away. "Opysis, let your king know immediately, by the time Maisie is dressed and ready, the sun will be rising," She walked out the door as she spoke, and Maisie rose.

"Well, since the walls are already in place, I will indeed go dress and you can let you King know the plan. We will meet at the gates at sunrise." Both emissaries rose and bowed to all of us.

"Thank you, Your Majesty, we are in your debt," Opysis said, before bowing once more and walking out with Solise.

Maisie began to walk towards the stairs when Kai grabbed her hand. "You were magnificent." He rose and kissed her before tossing her over his shoulder and carrying her up the stairs.

"We ssshould go, asss well, or Kai will keep her busssy and not let her dress," I mumbled under my breath.

Sic and Zugo both rose along with me and Sic laughed. "You're probably right. Let's go."

Kai put me down in the closet and slid up close to my chest. "Wanna quickie?" He slid his hands down to my ass and rubbed himself on me.

"Is that all you think about, Kai?" I asked, while laughing.

"Gods, no. I think about making love to you slowly and fucking you for hours until you scream the roof down. I think about watching you suck my cocks while I pull your hair." He paused and kissed me before smiling. "I also think about you pissing on my cocks." This last part was whispered so softly, I almost missed it. "See, I have other thoughts, too."

I laughed as I pushed him away. "We do need to help the Nymphs, though. maybe once we have dealt with my father and Salima we can spend days doing just that."

He grinned at me and then slapped my ass as I turned to walk away. "Promise?"

"Yes, Kai, I promise, but you will have to let the others be involved as well," I said, while looking through my clothes. I pulled out a pair of jeans and a shirt, while Kai pulled out matching lace undies and a bra. He dangled them in front of me and I snatched them from his hands.

"Just thinking about you in those will make my day a *hard* one." I rolled my eyes as I slipped them on, only to realize the panties were crotchless and the bra had holes where my nipples sat. Sic walked in and froze as I looked at Kai in exasperation.

"Really, Kai?" Sic said, as I sighed and began pulling my pants on.

"Admit that it's hot and you wanna fuck the hell out of her again," Kai said, as he turned to Sic.

"Don't need to admit shit to you. Now go." Sic kicked Kai out of the closet before apologizing. "You don't have to wear those if you don't want to. I'm sorry for his behavior."

"It's fine, besides, they are kinda comfy." I pulled my shirt on and the soft fabric teased my nipples, hardening them to peaks. "Do you think I look okay to help the Nymphs?" I asked nervously.

His smile soothed those nerves. "You look perfect. Let's go help them get settled in." We walked back out, and down the stairs once more. The doors opened and I noticed the red sun just skimming the Northern horizon. Kai and Emot had two unicorns packed with supplies that we might need, as Zugo held a third one attached to a wagon, and several large baskets piled in the back.

"We will be walking with the Nymphs today so it might take longer, but they walk fast and have no limit to their stamina, so if needed you can ride in the wagon," Sic spoke softly, as we made our way to the main gates, and the waiting Nymphs.

Sic hadn't been kidding about their speed, even the children walked faster than me. I lasted about a mile up the path

196

before climbing into the wagon with Zugo. We chatted for a bit about nothing until he went quiet. "Can I ask you a question?"

I looked at him, his face was a bit red in a cute kinda way. If I blushed as cute as he did, I'm fairly sure the guys would always have me blushing. "Sure, what's on your mind?" He worried his bottom lip while he thought for a moment.

"I was thinking about the other night and had a chat with Emot about stuff. Well, would you be willing to..." He trailed off and looked back ahead at the trail.

"Do what, Zugo? you can ask me. No one is around to hear, and I swear, I won't tell anyone if that makes you feel better."

"Peg me?" his mumbled words sounded almost silent, like he was afraid of my reaction.

"You want me to do it?" I asked softly, scooting closer to him on the seat. "You don't want one of the guys to do it?"

"No, I want you to do it," He admitted, and I put my hand on his thigh.

"I don't know how, but if you're willing to let one of the others teach me, then I'm willing to try." He seemed more comfortable with Emot, and I didn't think he would mind if Emot watched.

"I'm okay with that, but not Sic or Kai. I would prefer Emot. He seems to be the most understanding," He whispered, and I looked up the trail to where the others were. Kai was walking backwards talking to Sic and Emot who walked side by side. Kai laughed at something while Emot pushed him. His hands gestured crudely, and I rolled my eyes.

"You may be right about Emot being the best choice. Kai would only goof around and Sic, while understanding, can be a bit intense." I slid my hand on his thigh and he covered it with his own. We held hands the rest of the way to the Gryphon glade, the silence more peaceful than before.

Once we reached the pasture, the Nymph children ran around and played, while the adults began setting up tree houses on the opposite side of the lake, so they didn't disturb the Gryphons. A few of the adult Gryphons came to investigate the activity before the babies made an appearance. Sic helped me down from of the cart and handed me several paper packages.

"Maybe you can keep the kids busy for a bit while the adults work." He kissed my cheek, before I ran off towards the Nymph kids. I opened one package and tossed some meat towards the baby Gryphons and began to hand chunks to the children. We sat in the tall grass as the Gryphons took food from our hands, the kids giggling as they enjoyed the Gryphons.

By the time we were out of meat, most of the tree houses were done. The kids had run off, bored after the novelty wore off. One of the adult Gryphons stood near me when I rose, so I held out the last piece of meat to it. It took the meat gently, before bowing its head to me.

As I watched, the Gryphons walked back into their forest, Kai slid his hands around my waist. "I have some meat for you, if you want it." I laughed but leaned my head back against his chest.

"It will just have to wait until we get back. Where is Emot? I have a question for him," I asked, turning out of Kai's grip. He pointed over to the far trees and I saw Emot and Sic speaking

with a small man with a crown. I assumed he was the Wood Nymph King.

"I was sent to get you. The King would like to speak to you," Kai admitted, while handing me a damp towel to clean my hands. I washed my hands with the cloth as we walked back towards the others.

Sic smiled as I neared and waved towards me. "Your Majesty, this is Her Majesty Margaret Day. Maisie this is His Majesty Pasther of the Wood Nymphs." He held his hand out and I placed mine in his.

Shaking my hand swiftly, he pulled me in for a hug. "Thank you so much for all you have done for us. It shall not be forgotten."

"It is my pleasure. I am glad we could find a suitable place for you," As soon as the words left my mouth, a buzzing sound began to fill the pasture. Pasther looked up and frowned.

"I wonder why the Cloud Nymphs have come." I looked up but didn't see anything until a small buzzing cloud touched the ground and transformed into a petite woman. She was just as naked as the other Nymphs and I began to seriously wonder if Nymphs even knew what clothes were.

"Your Majesties, I have been sent by the Queen of the Cloud Nymphs. Salima has begun amassing an army and marching towards the Southern Kingdom." Sic swore when she finished, and she bowed. "I am so glad you found refuge here Pasther, my Queen will be relieved to know you are safe."

Sic looked at the woman and asked, "Do you need refuge as well?"

"Oh, no, we live in the clouds, so we are safe from all but dragons and they don't bother us since we are so small, and across a sea." She laughed at that and then I began to hear the buzzing again. "I need to be off. we will keep you posted if anything changes, Your Majesties." She bowed swiftly and then shrunk back down, a cloud forming around her body. The cloud sped off and I watched her head back southwest.

"Well, it looks like you should be going, I suspect you will have more people arriving in search of safety. Again, thank you for letting us live here, we shall treat the Gryphons well." Pasther shook Sic's hand while the others began packing up the wagon. He pulled me in for a hug and then said, "Please come visit whenever you want."

"Thank you, I shall." We waved to the Nymphs as Sic and Emot climbed up into the wagon. The other two unicorns no longer carried supplies, so we could ride back. Zugo climbed up onto one while Kai took the other and then held his hand out to me. He pulled me up in front of him and then we began to ride home.

30

Maisie

Kai flirted with me the entire ride back, making pun after pun about riding his cocks. Most made Zugo and I laugh but the laughter faded as we reached the castle's main gates. More families were arriving and Jeca was desperately trying to calm the crowd of his people. Cobra was working on more homes in the village which was quickly becoming overcrowded.

We dismounted and began to help those most in need. Many lived on the border with the Western Kingdom. Sic healed any who needed it and by the time the sun began to set, most of the people were in homes. One man stood off to one side waiting for the mass of bodies to clear and then Sic saw him.

"Fuck, what does he want?" He hissed softly, and I looked closer at the man. He looked so much like Sic, I thought I was seeing double, then I noticed the grey hair.

With the crowd gone, the man walked up and spoke softly. "May we speak, brother?" Sic nodded and we walked up towards the castle. Kai and Emot noticed and began making their way toward the gates pulling Zugo along with them.

"Maisie, this is my brother, Sunzi. He is the oldest of us," Sic spoke, as we walked through the gates. Sunzi placed his hand on his chest and bowed.

"It is an honor to meet you, Your Majesty." We continued on into the great hall, waiting for the others to arrive. Once everyone was seated, or standing around in Sic's case, Sunzi began. "Mother has begun attacking the Southern Kingdom. I have warned what towns I could, and many have gone underground. But those who haven't, will most likely seek refuge here. The others who are old enough are helping to warn people, but mother has the entire Western Army marching."

Sic paced and swore as his brother spoke. I hadn't seen him this agitated before. He wasn't even this bad when he was threatening to leave. "There is more Sicrin, and it isn't good. You might want to sit down for this one."

Sic paled slightly and sat as Sunzi suggested. "What could be worse than her attacking our allies?" His question was softer than I expected it to be, given his agitated state.

"Suanseh, Shezha, and Seku are all dead. Mother killed them and then ran off," Sunzi said, and Sic's face went white.

"Who are Suanseh, Shezha, and Seku?" I askedEmot, who was next to me softly. I didn't want to interrupt, but wanted to know.

"They are Sic's unmated baby brothers, who were still living with Salima at the citadel," He whispered back, and I felt my eyes bugging out.

"Who kills children?" I asked the table, as a tear began to roll down his cheek. "Why would she kill her own children?" my question was quiet, and Sunzi was the one who answered.

"We don't know why she killed them, we do, however, know she is planning on breeding a new mate. She has been showing signs of clutching soon, I would say in about two weeks,

she has already shed her pre-laying skin." I felt the horrified look cross my face.

"Pre-laying skin?" I asked in disgust.

Sic reached out a hand and I grasped it. "Females shed their skin about two to three weeks before laying eggs." His emotionless explanation was just that until he turned to Sunzi. "If she is about to lay, she will most likely fertilize them with Vago's seed, making them his."

"Eww, creepy evil half siblings," I whispered, and Sic actually laughed at that.

"I wanted you to hear it from me before word got to you. The others know and Sanouc took their bodies for a proper burial. We will wait until after the looming war and then give them the honor they deserve." Sic nodded his agreement and rose from the table.

"Thank you Sunzi, and please let the others know, if they need anything, to come here." Sunzi stood as well and then walked around to Sic. He pulled Sic into a tight hug for several moments, both needing the comfort only a brother could provide.

"I will see myself out. Please take care of yourself, and your family. We need this peace more now than ever." He bowed to the room and looked at me. "It was a pleasure. My dear, and I hope next time will be under better circumstances," With that, Sunzi walked out the castle door.

Once Sunzi left, Sic turned and swiped a hand across the side table sending the contents shattering to the ground. Glass slid across the floor as he stomped out. I rose to follow, but Kai held me back by the waist. "Don't, trust me. Let Emot handle it. Give him a day or two." Emot followed Sic up the stairs, as Kai pulled

me out the front doors, leaving Zugo standing in the great room alone.

"Let's go for a walk. we can go to the glade, get some more mimic plants." Kai held my hand while we walked out of the front gates, but I stalled, pulling him to a stop.

"Kai, Sic just lost his brothers. We can't just run off and have a good time while he is suffering."

"Please don't take this wrong, but Sic won't want you around right now. When his dad died, he punched me so hard I blacked out, and that isn't easy to do. His grief shows up in the form of rage, so by going out and having fun, I'm keeping you safe, and he will appreciate that more than you realize," He explained, as he pulled me in for a hug. "He knows you want to be with him, but the only person he will tolerate right now is Emot, and Emot is fast enough to dodge anything. So, let's go gather a few more mimic plants, I have an idea to decorate your bathroom."

We started back down the path and around the town and through the woods. I almost hummed 'to grandmother's house we go' but decided that would be in poor taste. The moon was full as always, and shone light on the path as we walked. Once we reached the open field, I walked towards the water and gazed at the silver reflection in the darkened gold. Kai held me tight from behind, for once not making sexual innuendos or puns.

"Jeca, be quiet, someone will hear us," I heard, what sounded like Cobra's voice, off through the trees.

"Please, I'm begging you," Jeca's voice whispered, and Kai pulled me back towards the trees behind us.

Without warning, the twins and Jeca spilled out into the far side of the clearing and Kai placed a hand over my mouth briefly. Whispering softly so no one would hear, "I think we should leave." I watched as Kai lifted me up slightly and began to silently make his way back to the path. Cobra and Viper pushed Jeca to the ground and I watched as each sat on a cock. Their bodies merged as they began to move, becoming one, just before we rounded the curve and I lost sight.

Once we were out of earshot, Kai walked faster until we reached the village. "Please tell me you didn't watch."

"I didn't see much, but they were both riding for a moment and then they merged. Then we rounded the corner and I didn't see anything else," I admitted, and he sighed while pinching the bridge of his nose. "What, I didn't see much."

"It's not that. Them merging is the only way for them to mate with anyone. In other words what we did. I don't mean sex, I mean, actually mate." He set me down and we began the walk back towards the castle.

"Is that a bad thing, if they make him happy?" I asked, not fully understanding why this was a bad thing.

"It isn't a bad thing, I just thought he would be over the whole mating thing after the disaster with my mother. I want him to be happy, I just hope they don't break his heart." He seemed genuinely concerned for his father's wellbeing and happiness. This was a side of Kai I very seldom saw, and I liked it.

"I have an idea, why don't we go back and make a mess of the kitchen? I'm starving." Kai smiled and picked me back up carrying me the rest of the way back.

Three Days Later

Sic didn't leave his room for three whole days. When he finally emerged, he seemed to have calmed down significantly. Emot had been kicked out that first night and hadn't been let back in, not even to give Sic food. He saw me in bed the morning he finally opened his door and sat on the edge of the bed.

"I'm sorry," He said, as he looked at me. "I shouldn't have shut you out."

Grabbing his hand, I squeezed his fingers. "I understand, Kai explained. Are you feeling a bit better?"

"She needs to be taken care of. I can't understand why she would do that to them. That's what haunts me the most, how could a mother kill her own children?" He spoke softly while looking at our hands, his thumb rubbing my knuckles.

"I don't know, but she will be dealt with, I promise. We will give them a proper burial and everything." I slid out of the covers and sat next to him. "I love you, Sic, and Emot loves you, and I know you are hurting, but we are here if you need us."

"What I need most right now is normalcy, at least until the time comes to deal with her. I heard more refugees have arrived," Just as he spoke, Kai walked out of his room and froze.

"You good, man?" Kai asked, looking at me and Sic very carefully.

"I'm good," Sic spoke as he rose, kissing my forehead. "You go back to sleep. Kai and I will take care of any new arrivals. Zugo and Emot can keep you company." He winked at Emot as his door opened, then pulled Kai out of the room, closing the doors behind them.

"Where isss he off to?" Emot asked, as he stood in his doorway.

"To help any new arrivals, he told me you and Zugo would keep me company for the day." Emot smirked at my words.

"I might have asssked him about sssomething before all thisss happened and he knowsss I haven't given it to you yet. Is Zugo up and are you in the mood to play?" He asked, as I arched a brow.

"What did you get?" I asked suddenly nervous.

"Nothing for you ssspecifically. I mean, you will ussse it, just not on yoursssself." He winked and walked back into his room. "You might want to go fressshen up a bit while I wake up Zugo," He called over his shoulder, so I slid from the bed and ran to the bathroom. It had been three days, and I was kinda curious about what he had planned.

When I walked out of the bathroom, Zugo was standing by the bed, his wide eyes glued to an open box before him. "Is everything okay?" I asked, and he nodded without looking up.

Emot pulled me towards the bed and slid my shirt off so I was standing naked by the foot of the bed. "You're in-charge love. Ssso, command away," Emot whispered into my ear.

"What am I doing?" I whispered back, but didn't need an answer. Zugo pulled a black leather belt out of the box, along with several different sized dildos, and a giant ass bottle of lube. "Ohhhh," Was all I could say, as Emot pulled off his pants. Zugo's own boxer pants were tented in the front, and I could see the nervous excitement in his eyes.

"Strip," I told Zugo, and he jerked, dropping the toys back in the box before rushing to strip. "On the bed, face down." He climbed on the bed and lay face down, and I looked at Emot with a 'what now' look.

Emot pulled the leather belt out of the box and two large dildos. Threading one through a hole in the bottom, he walked over to me and helped me step into the leather. The large dildo hung heavily from the front of the belt. He helped me onto the bed before pushing me on top of Zugo. The dildo just rubbed Zugo ass crack and he shivered below me.

Emot pushed my legs apart and then I felt the blunt head of the second dildo slip through a hole in the belt and slowly into my slit. He fastened it into place before pulling me back up and smiling as it moved within me. He knelt next to me and shifted his cocks to one. Grasping the base, he began to instruct me. "Grab the bassse of the dildo and line it up with his assss, make sssure you ussse lotsss of lube and go ssslow at firssst. Got it?"

I nodded as he handed me the bottle of lube and crawled towards the head of the bed leaning against it so he could watch. "Zugo, on all fours," I commanded, and he responded immediately, climbing to all fours. "Crawl forward until Emot's

cock is in your face." I wanted Zugo to at least watch as Emot stroked himself, Emot liked that and Zugo seemed to, as well.

I slowly followed, the dildo in my pussy exciting me more. Doing as Emot instructed, I used a lot of lube on the dildo, even swirling several fingers around Zugo's ring. I pressed one in and slowly readied him for more, then slipped a second one in. Thrusting several times, he groaned in pleasure and begged for more. The sound of begging made me wetter. Adding a third finger he moaned, and I watched Emot stroking his cock right in Zugo's face.

"Are you ready?" I asked, and he begged for more as I slid my fingers out. Just to be safe I added even more lube to the head of the dildo and did as Emot instructed. Grabbing the base, I lined it up and began to press in. Zugo rocked a bit helping the head breach his tight ring. Once the head was in, I paused to give him time to adjust.

He began to press back, and I knew he was ready for more, so I inched forward and back slipping more of the dildo in each time. By the time the dildo was fully seated, he was moaning with each stroke. My own body was on fire from the dildo deep in my pussy. Each move I made on Zugo, made the one in me move too. I slowly began to stroke in and out fully, bringing pleasure to Zugo and I both.

Emot watched with hooded eyes as he stroked himself at the same pace as I worked. I slid my hand up Zugo's back and pulled his hair until he arched up more. "Do you want to suck a cock while I fuck your ass?" I hissed into his ear, while continuing to thrust my hips. He nodded his head as much as my grip allowed, until I pushed his head back down. "Suck his cock," I commanded, and Emot paused his strokes.

He shifted back to two cocks while climbing onto his knees. "Let'sss ssstart with one," His words were for Zugo, as I began to speed up just a bit. While I watched, Zugo tentatively licked the head of one of Emot's cocks. "That'sss it, now sssuck the head." Emot held himself still while I held Zugo's hips thrusting. Zugo captured Emot's cock between his lips just as I slid out and he moaned around Emot. The picture before me was so hot, I began to feel my body tighten around the dildo. Zugo sucked more of Emot into his mouth and then pulled back onto the dildo in his ass.

Zugo began to rock on all fours, taking Emot and then sliding back again. I held his hips, adding a small thrust as he pushed back. His rocking increased more as I slid my hands down and began to stroke his cocks. The sounds Zugo was making made me want to make him cum over and over. Emot watched as I fucked Zugo's ass and held Zugo's hair as he sucked.

Emot growled softly and began to pull out of Zugo's mouth but Zugo wouldn't release him. "I'm gonna cum, let me pull out."

"Swallow his cum, Zugo," I commanded, and Emot's eyes shot to mine. "He wanted to suck your cock, so let him at least get the full experience." Emot shrugged and thrust a few more times into Zugo's mouth as Zugo's cocks began to twitch in my hands. Emot groaned, shooting cum on the bed with one cock while Zugo swallowed the cum from the other. Zugo's cocks pulsed as his orgasm raced through him, coating my hands in the process. His body clamped down onto the dildo in his ass and I couldn't move until his orgasm passed.

Emot collapsed back against the headboard, as Zugo wobbled on all fours. I slid the dildo out of his ass, and he collapsed onto the bed beside Emot's legs. My own body ached at not getting its own release as I pulled the strap on off. I tossed

everything back in the box just as Emot pulled me into his lap. "You didn't get off, love," He held me close, as he spoke softly.

"It's okay, this wasn't about me. It was for Zugo," I mumbled against his neck.

"That'sss not how thisss worksss, though. Sssee, you are sssupposed to get off too," He said, while turning me slightly, so I sat sideways in his lap. His finger trailed down my chest to swirl around my nipples before traveling on towards my clit. "Let'sss get you nice and wet before I fuck you." Zugo was on his side watching Emot play with my body, his tongue wetting his lips in anticipation. Emot laid me down on my side so my head was by Zugo's feet until Zugo slid down the bed more. I felt a pair of fingers tease my slit just as Zugo's tongue hit my clit. Emot lifted my top leg onto his arm as his fingers slid deep angling them to hit my g-spot.

Between the two of them, the orgasm I had been denied swiftly rushed back up and I cried out as I spasmed around Emot's digits. The bed dipped and I felt Emot's cocks line up with both my ass and pussy, all the while Zugo's tongue flicked my clit. My moan was loud in the room as Emot crept into my body, rubbing every nerve. Zugo's cocks slowly rose and I realized how easily it would be for me to suck him. Emot must had realized the direction of my thoughts, because he pulled Zugo closer to us and held his cocks for me.

I sucked first one's head and then the other, holding the bases with my hands. The harder I sucked the harder his tongue worked on my clit. Emot began thrusting as I took both of Zugo's heads into my mouth at once, and I moaned around him. Emot fucked me while I sucked both of Zugo's cocks swirling my tongue between them. "Godsss, you look hot with two cocksss in your mouth," Emot whispered, as he increased his pace. My body began to tighten around him as he stroked faster, Zugo's tongue

flicking as fast as possible. Zugo's cocks pulsed slightly and I knew he was getting as close as I was. Emot rolled his hips just right and I came, flooding Zugo's face and the base of Emot's cocks in the process.

Zugo moaned as his cocks shot cum into my mouth, and Emot pulsed deep in my pussy. I swallowed as much of Zugo's cum as I could, but I could feel it dribbling out the sides. When I finally released him, more cum slid down my chin. Emot turned my head and licked my chin clean before kissing me deeply. Once he pulled back, he smiled. "You look sssexy with cum dripping down your face. What I wouldn't give to watch the othersss cum on your face." I felt my body relax and he slipped free, pulling out and curling around my back. Zugo rotated around so his head was by mine, his grin said exactly how happy he was. He pressed his lips to mine before wrapping an arm over my waist.

"I think I love you, Maisie," He whispered before dozing off, and my heart melted.

"I know I love you, Zugo," I whispered, and Emot's head peeked over my shoulder.

"Do you love me?" He asked softly.

I turned so I could look him in the eyes. "Of course, I love you, Emot. I probably should tell you all more often how I feel." He kissed the corner of my mouth, and then wrapped his arm around me the same way Zugo's was, sandwiching me between two of my loves. Only one thing would make this better, and that was Kai and Sic being here, too. Emot's breathing slowed as he dozed off and I closed my eyes, just enjoying the warmth.

The day wore on with more refugees arriving, and each one looked worse than the last. Seeing mothers with injured children in the wake of my mother's actions hurt, but the injured women hurt more. I saw Maisie's face in each one and realized that they were someone's mother, mate, or a lover. The idea of Maisie suffering the way these women had, made my blood boil. It was difficult to imagine a life without her at this point, but I realized I would gladly die to protect her from suffering the way her people had.

Kai was helping Viper get supplies to the people, while Cobra and I helped the injured. Jeca bounced back and forth between the two, running to get things when needed and generally helping out. At one point, I noticed Cobra's blush when he walked away and decided to poke a bit. "So, Jeca has been awfully helpful today, I wonder why?"

Cobra's blush was instant, and she looked at me for a moment, before focusing back on the man she was healing. "These are his people along with Evat's. Evat has been just as helpful to the new arrivals, as well as Escu." She attempted to change the subject, but I caught her glancing in his direction once again.

"Yes, but you have been staring at him a lot," I spoke, as the man left heading towards Viper and Kai, for supplies.

She turned to glare at me. "What do you want?"

"I just want to know what's going on. I'm well aware of the fact that Kai's parents weren't in love. What I wanna know is, are you?" I didn't beat around the bush and it helped to take my mind off my mother's actions.

"Fine, if you must know, yes. Happy now?" She hissed, as more people streamed through the gates.

"What about Viper?" I cautiously asked, and saw her blush even more. "You two mated him, didn't you?" I guessed, and her eyes looked like saucers as she looked at me.

"Don't tell Kai yet, please. Jeca didn't want to wait, in case something happened to him, but he doesn't want to tell Kai until things have settled," She begged me as she began helping a young woman with a nasty bump on the head.

I waited until she finished checking her over, and then whispered, "Kai already knows. He and Maisie were in the mimic grove the night you three were out there. They left before anything happened, but Kai said Maisie saw you two merge." Her face went pale and I smiled to reassure her. "I don't think he minds, he seemed happy for his dad. A bit grossed out, but happy."

She snorted a laugh just as Jeca began to walk back over. "What are you two laughing about?" I watched Cobra pull Jeca away for a moment and then he barked his own laughter. He kissed Cobra for all to see and I noticed Kai's exaggerated gag from across the open area. Viper smacked his arm and he laughed before going back to work.

It felt almost good to be doing the normal things again. I know there would come a time when we would have to grieve but with so much work to be done, it helped numb the pain. Maisie, Emot and Zugo arrived outside just after the sun reached its highest point and I could see the joy on her face. I had known that she was worried about me and that I had kept her alone at night, but I wasn't her only mate, and she needed to remember that.

Emot and Zugo were joking around as they walked past me to help Kai and Viper. Maisie stopped at my side and began wrapping bandages and tidying our makeshift hospital table. I reached out and grabbed her hand, turning her to face me. Pulling her around, I wrapped her in a tight hug and kissed the top of her head.

"What was that for?" She asked looking up at me, while she wrapped her arms around my back.

"For reminding me that there is still a life to live. You do need to remember, though, that you do have four mates, you can't just focus on me," I tried not to sound harsh as I spoke the last part.

"I know, but you need me right now, and they understand that. They love you just as much as I do, just in a different way," She said, and I looked over at the others as they worked alongside Viper. "Kai sees you as a brother, while Zugo sees you as a father figure, and Emot, well, he loves you like I love you." She reached up on tiptoes and pressed her lips to mine. "Now, let's get these people patched up and sent to their new homes." She pulled out of my arms and began to work on tidying the table once more. I watched her work for several moments, realizing how lucky I was.

The sun set as we walked back towards the castle, several guards were helping the last few stragglers that came through the gates. I had a sinking suspicion that tomorrow was going to be another busy day. It had been a week, or four days, since Sic's brother had come and each day more people arrived looking for shelter. I yawned as I stepped through the doors and decided to skip dinner in favor of a long hot bath.

The walk up the stairs felt like climbing a mountain, and by the time I opened the bathroom door, I was exhausted. I sat on the edge of the tub and turned the water on and then stoppered the drain. While I waited for the tub to fill, I stood and stripped, and midstrip I noticed several mimic plants sitting along the windows. Each plant was potted, and each one looked like a penis.

"KAI!" I yelled, and the door slowly swung open to reveal his grinning face.

"Do you like your decorations?" He laughed and I realized Emot was behind him laughing his ass off.

"Why would you decorate my bathroom with dicks?" I asked, as he closed the door on Emot.

"Well, we wanted to decorate it for you, and we figured the bathroom was the perfect place for dicks. Well, besides your pussy that is." I rolled my eyes as he pulled me towards the plants. "These two are Sic's, these are Emot's, Zugo's, and the most impressive ones are mine." He pointed to the last two plants, and grinned.

Each window had two plants, one was a single dick, the other was a double. "How did you even convince the others to do it?" I asked, as I pulled my pants off.

"Well they saw the pair of boobs in my room and wanted their own. I said maybe if you got a few mimics of them, you might be willing to give them their own. Zugo is the one who suggested doing both, separate and together." Walking back to the tub I checked the level while Kai watched me. "So, would you make them some?"

I climbed over the edge of the tub and sat down, checking the level of water before turning it off. "I guess, tit for tat after all." Kai walked past me and opened the door.

"SHE SAID YES!" He yelled, and I heard a few shouts of joy and one, 'leave her alone' from Sic.

Emot pulled Kai through the door and then popped his head in. "Enjoy your bath." He closed the door softly and I leaned back in the water to relax. The heat loosened my tight muscles and soothed my aches from the day. I was looking forward to finally taking on my father, but with so many people in need still, I hadn't even been able to plan on how. Thirty minutes passed while I sat in the bathtub, and the water was lukewarm when I pulled the plug and rose.

Wrapping a towel around myself to dry off, I opened the door to a pitch-black bedroom. "Thanks guys, you could have left a light on for me," I mumbled, only to have a match flare to life.

The match died out as a single candle was lit on the side table. I walked towards the bed using the light to guide my steps and saw all four of the guys in my bed. "What is this, a slumber party?" I asked, while standing by the side of the bed.

"Maybe?" Kai said, and Sic pulled me onto the mattress and his chest.

"You can have the middle," He said before he kissed me, then passed me to Emot.

"We wanted to sssleep with you tonight," Emot whispered, as he rolled me towards the middle of the bed. Zugo leaned over Kai and pressed a kiss to my lips before settling back into his place.

Then Kai rolled me to face him. "Sweet dreams, sugar." He pressed his lips to mine and slid his hand down to the edge of the towel and pulled it free. The cool air felt good on my skin for a moment, then they pulled the covers up and cool sheets covered me. I could feel all of Kai's body pressed against me, then Emot rolled towards my back and I felt every inch of him, as well. The warmth, of having all four guys in the bed, lulled me into a dreamless sleep.

I woke in the middle of the night to an empty bed, then noticed Sic and Kai were standing by the doorway. I didn't see Zugo or Emot anywhere. I sat up just as Kai closed the door and turned back towards the bed. He saw me sitting up in bed and crawled up the bottom when he reached it. Sic whispered, "I'm

getting dressed to go help Emot and Zugo." Kai waved a hand as he pulled me back down into the sheets.

"Why are you up, sugar?" He asked, as he pulled me into his chest.

I cuddled closer to his warmth, before answering, "I don't know. What's going on, where are the others?"

"Do you really want to talk about that right now or would you rather I help you back to sleep?" I gave him a look that said, 'stop avoiding the subject and answer me'. "Zugo and Emot are helping more refugees that arrived about an hour ago. Sic is going out to help them."

"Why didn't you wake me. I would have helped." He nervously looked away for a second. "These are different refugees. They are deserters from the North and West armies. Many refused to fight for Vago or Salima, so it was run or die. They are being set up in the barracks for now, but Cobra and Viper are weeding out those who truly want peace and are willing to fight for you, if needed. Thuzo is adding those to the royal guard, and the others are your army."

"Wait, I have an army?" He smiled as he rolled me on top of him.

"Yes, you have an army, it was very small until the East and South armies joined you." He kissed me trying to distract me from the fact that I have the ability to fight Vago when the time comes.

"Why wasn't I told? I have been racking my brain for days now, trying to figure out how to defeat Vago." I rolled off him and sat up.

"Because the truth is, you would need the West army as well to defeat him, and with Salima on Vago's side, we don't stand a chance yet. The more people from their armies that defect to us, the better we are, but we must be careful of spies, that's why we didn't wake you, we don't want you anywhere near these people until we know who is being truthful or and who isn't." He sat up and tipped my chin, so he was looking me in the eyes. "Our number one priority is keeping you safe, even if that means our deaths." He pressed his lips to mine softly, while pulling me closer.

"Kai, do you really think now is the time?" I whispered, as he broke our kiss.

"I'm here, you're here. I'm on 'keep Maisie happy and safe' duty, so we could go into my room and I can show you my new sheets." He slid his hand down my back and squeezed my ass.

"What new sheets would those be?" My curiosity gets the better of me. I knew I should focus on what was happening in the world, but my brain chose that moment to focus on other things.

Kai rose from the bed, pulling me with him, his robe falling open in front to reveal his cocks. "Follow me, I promise, you won't be disappointed." Tugging my hand, he led me to his doorway and then swung the door wide open. Kai flipped a switch and waved me in. He closed the door and locked it, before walking to the head of the bed. "Ready?" I nodded, and he pulled the bedspread off to reveal black sheets.

"Is that it, black sheets?" He laughed and pulled me closer to the bed.

"Feel." I slid my hand across the top and realized they felt odd, not exactly fabric but I couldn't put my finger on it. "If I told

you they were waterproof would that help?" His whisper was right behind me, and I shivered in excitement.

"Why would we need waterproof sheets?" I could hear the coyness in my voice, as he began to rub himself on me.

"I can think of several reasons, lube wrestling, making you cum so much the bed wouldn't dry for months, watersports, the options are endless. So wanna snake wrestle?" He wrapped his arms around me and flopped us onto the bed. "Oops."

"You are such a flirt, Kai," I chided, but he just laughed as he rolled us, so I was pinned beneath him.

"But you love it, and me." His cheeky grin said he knew as much. I felt his cocks pressed between my legs and opened mine wider to accommodate his hips. Pulling his robe off his shoulders, I tugged until he was just as naked as I was. He rose for a moment to toss it to the side and I wiggled into the center of his bed. He climbed fully on and followed me on all fours. "But what to do with this yummy snake in my bed." He licked my thigh as he crawled higher. He paused and looked up my body, his mouth inches from where I wanted him.

"Did I say snake? I meant snack," As soon as the words left his mouth, he flicked his tongue along my slit. I arched into his mouth as he licked and flicked his tongue along my slit. He sucked hard on my clit and I moaned before he rose up again. "Roll over," He whispered softly, and I rolled so I was on my stomach.

He picked up my hips just a bit, pinning my legs between his. My face was still on the bed as I felt both his cocks line up with my slit. He rocked his way in and the tightness, aided by my legs being closed, rubbed all sorts of nerves. My body greedily accepted both his cocks and I began to beg for more as he started

to move. "I'm not letting you out of this bed until you can't walk. I'm gonna do every dirty little thing you want me to do." I moaned as he rubbed my g-spot just right.

He stroked me several times, and then paused deep inside me. "This is why I got the sheets," He whispered, and I began to feel wet heat flooding my pussy. The idea that he was doing this in a bed was so taboo and erotic that it sent me over the edge. I cried out as pleasure raced along my nerves, and he began to thrust again. "That's my girl, cum on my cocks."

His chest was on my back as he kissed my shoulder. "Kai." I moaned as he began to speed up, my body enjoying each thrust but needing more. He rolled over pulling me on top of his chest, but not letting me sit up. He pounded up into me as he pulled my legs wide. The change in angle had him rubbing my g-spot harder and I felt my body begin to race towards a second release.

He pounded into me sending me, flying as I flooded his cocks. "That's it, get me nice and wet," His words hissed softly in my ear, and I moaned as he sped up even more. Pushing me upright so I could hold myself up on my hands, I noticed a mirror on the wall. "Did you see my mirror?" He asked as he opened his legs, so I had a clear view of his cocks disappearing into my pussy.

I couldn't look away as he slowed his thrust, pulling out before sliding back all the way back in. It was like watching live porn, and it was hot. He sped up again and I watched as I came again, my body's spasming pushed his cocks together and he groaned. "Isn't it a beautiful sight? Your body swallowing mine, over and over," He spoke, as he continued to thrust.

My arms began to wobble so he paused and sat up behind me, supporting me from behind. His lips kissed my neck and earlobe before he whispered. "I wanna watch us fuck for days, but we don't have that kinda time right now. So, I'll settle for watching you piss on my cocks and a few more orgasms," His words sent chills of pleasure up my spine and I relaxed as much as I could. He paused his thrusts until he saw me start in the mirror and then he began to pound into me as hard as possible.

I watched the excitement on his face as my body let go, and I screamed as I came around him. He kept working me fast and hard until I orgasmed two more times in rapid succession. My orgasms set him off, making him roar softly as his cocks pulsed deep in me, my body clamping his into place. He wrapped his arms around me and rolled us to the side so we could both be comfortable until my body released his.

"I love you, Kai," I whispered, as my body began to drift off into sleep.

"I love you too, sugar. Get some sleep." He pressed a kiss to my hair, and I began to doze off, our bodies still locked together.

When I woke up, I realized that Kai was still wrapped around my back, his cocks still buried in my body. He must have remained awake, because he felt me move. "You have to relax, sugar, I'm still stuck tight."

"What do you mean you're still stuck?" I asked, realizing at the same moment that my body was still locked around his. "How do I relax?"

"Just focus on relaxing your muscles," He spoke calmly, while running a hand slowly over my side.

Closing my eyes, I willed my body to relax, but it just wouldn't. I began to try again, just as a knock sounded on the door. A key slid into the lock and clicked just as Kai tossed the top sheet over us. Sic walked in with Cobra following close behind, and my face went beet red. "You could have called out." Cobra looked at us and I buried my face in the mattress, hoping to just disappear. She handed me a small vial and told me to drink up. "It will help with your current situation, I promise."

I threw back the vial and a sweet lemony flavor washed over my tongue. My body instantly relaxed and Kai sighed as he slid out. Cobra walked towards the door and tossed back as she walked out, "Have fun with that one."

"What did that mean?" I asked, and Sic chuckled softly.

"Nothing that we can't handle. Typically, you don't get stuck that long unless breeding is taking place. But I doubt that's what happened," Sic's words made me bolt upright, and Kai laughed softly.

"Sugar, when you lock up like that, it makes us cum. Staying locked for hours makes us cum over and over. I lost count after six." Kai slid to the side of the bed and pulled me close.

"Oh, Gods, that has to be painful after a while," I said, as I slowly slid to the edge, an odd jiggly feeling in my legs.

"We are designed for it, so it doesn't hurt. It got a bit annoying to lay there while your body sucked mine dry, though. If only because I wanted to cuddle and sleep. You making me cum every twenty minutes was not conducive to sleep," He joked as he stood, his cocks looked bruised in places. "I'm fine," He said, noticing the direction of my gaze.

"Come, let's get you washed up and dressed. More people are arriving, and we need the extra hands." Sic helped me stand but my legs gave out the instant he let go. He caught me again and swore. "Kai help her shower and I'll get clothes." With that, Kai scooped me up and walked us to his bathroom.

We showered swiftly, making sure to clean well before Sic came back with my clothes. Sic wrapped a towel around me and carried me to the small chair. He dried me off and my legs began to tingle. "Why are my legs asleep?" I whispered, as he helped me put the pants on and then a shirt.

"Cobra gave you Devil's Hare's Fairymoss. It's a potion mainly used for birthing mothers, almost like an epidural of sorts. The added benefit is that it relaxes everything from waist down, so it relaxed your legs too. It doesn't last long, usually about thirty minutes, so you should be right as rain soon." Once I was dressed, Sic scooped me up and began to carry me out. Kai was dressing as we left. "See you outside in a few," Sic yelled, as we walked through the door.

Sic carried me downstairs and put me back on my feet. The tingles were now pins and needles, as I waited for the feeling to return once more. Evat walked through the castle doors with Emot and Escu following behind him.

"Your Majesty, I am sorry to disturb you, but the last of the refugees from the Eastern Kingdom have arrived. They wished to speak with all of you." I nodded and tried a tentative step. I was able to support my weight once more, so I walked slowly towards the door. Sic let me hold his arm as a safety net, as Kai raced down the stairs. We all walked back out into the yard where a young couple waited.

Emot smiled at the couple and introduced us, "This is my brother Ezet, and his new wife Arinsa." I shook both of their hands and realized that Ezet looked almost the same age as Emot. He noticed my looks and Escu laughed softly.

"Emot was the first to hatch out of three eggs. Ezet was the last of the three, and their clutch mate Esen was in the middle," Escu spoke up.

"I thought only one egg hatched at a time." I looked at her and she smiled in her motherly way.

"I tell you what, we shall have a nice girl talk later." I nodded once, before switching back to the reason Ezet was here.

"Please speak freely," I indicated to Ezet, and he nodded, his face turning grim.

"We got out as many as we could, but Vago has completely taken over the Eastern Kingdom. Many are still trapped there, but most are in hiding. Esen currently has our army boarding your wall for added safety for this area. We suspect that once he has control of the Southern and Western Kingdoms, he will bring attacks on the central lands." I frowned and looked at Sic.

"My brothers have already reported that Salima and Vago are working together. She has begun to attack the Southern Kingdom and I suspect that once she has control, they will work together towards us. We need a plan, and fast," Sic relayed the information that he knew, as Jeca arrived with Viper and Cobra.

"Why don't we go inside and begin working on a plan, we know he will eventually attack us. We need to figure out where the most likely place will be. We also need to work on any ideas for a peaceful resolution to this conflict," I spoke up, and began walking back into the castle, unaided this time. Everyone began to follow me back inside to begin planning for Vago's eventual attack and the potential war looming on the horizon.

After hours of planning and trying to come up with contingencies, everyone felt somewhat prepared for the worst possible outcome. We were walking back outside when a Cloud Nymph landed in the castle yard, transforming into another naked woman. She bowed to all of us. "Your Majesties, my Queen wished me to tell you, that the Southern Kingdom has fallen to the West. The remaining Southern Army is currently stationed at the mountain pass guarding the gate there." I looked at Jeca and Sic and Jeca frowned.

"I will go with the twins and get the Army inside the gate to guard the pass. Kai's brothers command the army so they should have remained loyal to us." Viper, Cobra and Jeca walked off swiftly, heading towards the mountain path.

"Evat, would you be willing to have your army enter the gates to protect it from the inside as well?" Sic asked and Evat began to walk off towards the gate that all the refugees had come through.

Ezet kissed his wife and left her with Escu. "I'll be back soon. You stay with Mother and be safe." He ran after his dad as she watched with a nervous look on her face.

The two women walked back around towards the Nymph Lake as the Cloud Nymph waited for everyone but the five of us to remain. "My Queen also wanted me to let the five of you know, that if it comes to war, the Cloud Nymphs will be on your side. We have the ability to hide your armies while your troops can still see. The Water Nymphs have also volunteered their help, their army is over two million strong, all highly skilled women. Ours is an additional two thousand skilled warriors. The Wood Nymphs have no army but offered to help those who are injured. My queen has also begun talks with Braceboro to gain the aid of the dragons, if necessary." She bowed once more, and I was stunned at the sheer number of warriors.

"Please tell your Queen we thank her, and if it comes to war, we appreciate the help," Sic diplomatically spoke, since I was still stunned silent.

"I shall convey the message, Your Majesties." She bowed one final time, shrunk into her cloud and zoomed away.

"Do you really think it will come to a war?" I asked the guys, as I watched her disappear into the sky.

"If it does, we can only hope that we outnumber Vago so much, it is over quickly, with as few casualties as possible," Zugo spoke up, and I looked over at him.

"Do you know how many people he has in his army?" I asked, hoping he might have some idea.

"The entire population of the Northern Kingdom is his army. Every man, woman, and child over the age of sixteen. But as far as actual numbers, I have no idea." Zugo's words made my heart sink in my chest. How could he make children fight for him? "You also need to understand that most of them are so

brainwashed by his propaganda that they will do anything for him.”

“Who do we know that can do some recon?” Emot asked the others.

“The only one I know is Viper but that would put her at risk, and I doubt Jeca will allow that, at this point,” I spoke, causing Emot and Zugo to look at me. Kai pretended to gag for fun as I filled them in. “Jeca mated with Cobra and Viper.” Emot’s eyebrows rose to his hairline and Zugo snorted a laugh.

“He’s too old for new mates if you ask me,” Kai said, but there wasn’t any conviction behind his words.

“What about Ahxezo and Yaga, would they know of any other people who could do reconnaissance?” I asked, and Sic smiled.

“We could always ask them, it couldn’t hurt.” I turned and headed across the yard towards their home and knocked on the door. The others followed me in, as the door swung open to Ahxezo’s smiling face.

“Come on in, my dear, I have been hoping you would come for a visit.” He walked into the kitchen to return with a plate of cookies and fresh tea, that still steamed. Yaga was snoozing in a chair by the fireplace.

“We came to ask if you know of anyone who could scout out the numbers of the Northern Army for us?” Kai asked, and Ahxezo paused in his pouring.

“I might know a few besides Yixe and Yoxe, but I highly doubt you will like my answers.” He handed cups around to us as he sat in his own chair.

"Why wouldn't we like your suggestions? We have money to pay for their services if need be," Sic spoke, before taking a sip and placing his cup on the table.

"Kreetik, Athargos, Aindreas Fade, and Scáthach - those four could easily determine the information you need," Ahxezo whispered, so only we could hear. Emot's face paled and Kai looked physically sick.

"You are suggesting the four deadliest people on this planet to aide us? they would just as soon kill us than help us," Sic replied, but Ahxezo shrugged.

"I told you, you wouldn't like it." He sipped his tea as if nothing was amiss.

"Who are they?" I asked. As soon as the question passed my lips the door slammed against the far wall and a beautiful woman stood in the doorway, surrounded by three men.

"Speak and we shall appear," Her words were melodic, and a sense of dread washed over me. Her bright green dress highlighted her knee length red hair, while her pale skin made her reddened eyes stand out on her slim face.

"This is Scáthach, a Banshee from Ecaniel. The other three are her men Kreetik, Athargos, and Aindreas Fade," Ahxezo spoke softly, as she nodded her head.

"What can we do for the Empress of Lasina?" She spoke again, and I suddenly felt like weeping.

"We are in need of information," Sic answered her question, just as tears began to roll down my cheeks.

Vago

I watched as my cock slid in and out of Salima's pussy hard and fast. She was bent over my desk, crying out with each thrust as I pulled her hair. "That's it cunt, take every fucking inch," My words caused a moan to slide past her lips and I bent forward more to wrap my other hand around her throat. "What have I said about making noises?"

"Only ones of pain, sir," She said, as I squeezed her neck tighter and she gasped for air. Her body tightened on mine and I pounded harder until I felt the rush of cum fill her pussy. I pulled out and dropped her onto the desk.

"Get dressed and then go," I spoke, as I tucked my unshifted dicks back into my pants.

"Vago, darling, I need to tell you something." I sighed in annoyance and waited for her to speak.

When she didn't begin right away, I yelled, "Well, what is it?" She walked up to me and slid her hand up my chest and around the back of my neck. Trying to pull me down for a kiss. Pulling her arm off, I glared at her.

"Fine, I wanted to tell you that I'll be laying in a few days. We're going to have children," The second the words left her

mouth, I snapped. My hand went back around her throat and I pushed her across my desk. "Yes, Vago, fuck me again," Her choked out words hardening my cocks, but I was pissed.

"Why would you think I would want more children, when I still have one I need to kill." Squeezing harder she gasped, and I unbuttoned my pants to ease the ache. Thank Gods, she hadn't laid them yet and they weren't fertilized, just empty shells at this point, but I wouldn't give her the opportunity to lay them.

"I just thought, now that Clara was dead, we could be officially married and rule this country together," Her words made me freeze, and rage began to simmer in my veins.

"Clara isn't dead, I left her alive." My hand loosened on her throat just enough for her to speak.

"Well, of course you left her alive, you couldn't be the one to kill her, or people would know. That's why I did it for you. She begged for her life as I sliced her over and over, leaving her to bleed out on Ear…" She bragged until the words were cut off as I squeezed more, and I lined my dick up with her twat.

"I left her alive because I still loved her, you cunt." I slammed in and she cried out in pain making me pulse. "Now, you're going to suffer." I held her pinned to my desk with my hand around her throat, her body loving the punishment. That is, until I pulled my knife out of its sheath.

I slid the blade around her breast softly at first, and then harder slicing through her pearly white skin. I repeated the action around her other breast, and she cried out in pain making me fuck her harder. "You won't live once I'm done fucking you." True fear entered her eyes at that point, as I began to slice her skin all over, blood pooling on my desk and dripping down the sides. She scratched at my hand that I had wrapped around her throat,

silently begging me not to kill her. Her mouth moved as she gasped for air, but none came, and she began to turn a beautiful shade of blue.

I squeezed her throat harder, feeling the fight leave her slowly, as the blood dripped out of the cuts. Her eyes rolled back and then her body went limp below me. I filled her pussy one last time as I squeezed even tighter and then heard the snap of her neck. I pulled out and wiped my dick off on her dress, then yelled out to a servant.

"Clean this mess up. I have a war to plan." I watched as her lifeless body was carried away and the maids began to clean up the blood. Once my office was back in order, I sat down and began plotting my next move.

Acknowledgements

Thank you to all my wonderful readers, I hope you enjoyed the first book of this series. The rest will be out soon.

Thank you to my wonderful Alpha readers, Teresa, Everly, Melody, Ira, and Cassy. This series has been a wild ride and I am grateful to you all for hanging on with both hands.

Mindy G and Krystal, I am truly grateful to have you both in my life; and I hope this series becomes a cherished one, snakes and all.

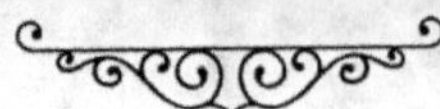

About the Author

Rozie Marshall is an inspired writer from Colorado, where she lives with her husband, kids, and fur babies. She has a BA in European History and works in a bookstore, where else? Although she started writing over a decade and a half ago, it took some convincing for her to publish her first book, but once it happened, the floodgates of words burst, and the books kept coming.

Often referred to by her fans as Goddess of Smut and All That is Sexy, she delights her fans with her special knack for kink and smut. When she is not busy arguing with her characters, she spends her time plotting new stories and doing research for her books. Oh, and coffee is her best friend.

You can find out more about Rozie Marshall and follow her updates by joining her Facebook Group and subscribing to her Newsletter.

Website: https://www.roziemarshall.com/

Facebook: https://www.facebook.com/RozieMashall/

Facebook Group:
https://www.facebook.com/groups/RozieMarshallBooks/

Follow me on Amazon:
https://www.amazon.com/author/roziemarshall

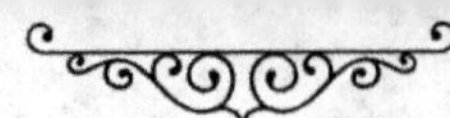

More by Rozie Marshall

Claimed by the Goddess Series

Triad Found – Available on Kindle Unlimited

Pentacle Bound – Available on Kindle Unlimited

Elements Tamed – Available on Kindle Unlimited

Goddess Claimed – Available on Kindle Unlimited

Magic Unleashed – Available on Kindle Unlimited

Eight Deadly Sins

Lilith's story will continue in Original Sin

Original Sin – Coming Soon

Love Bites

Bite of My Life Prequel – Available on Kindle Unlimited

Sisters of the Seven Seas

Silver Sails – Available on Kindle Unlimited

The Lasina Chronicles

The Basilisk Princess – Available Wide

The Basilisk Queen – Available Wide

The Basilisk Empress – Available Wide

Personal Harem Series

Red's Rangers – Available on Kindle Unlimited

Fallen Petals – Available on Kindle Unlimited

Brothel of the Damned

Cowritten with C.T. Dracass, & Melody Calder

Deadly Desires – <u>Available on Kindle Unlimited</u>

Deadly Liaison – <u>Available on Kindly Unlimited</u>

Anthologies

Anonymous: A BDSM Anthology

Anonymous Part 2: A BDSM Anthology

The Devil's Playground

Stand Alone

Twisted & Torn: A Dragon's Tail – <u>Available on Kindle</u>

A Thief's Lover – <u>Available on Kindle</u>